# THE REPLACEMENT
by
Ronald F. Lazenby

*The Replacement*

Trilogy Christian Publishers A Wholly Owned Subsidary of Trinity Broadcasting Network

2442 Michelle Drive Tustin, CA 92780

Copyright © 2021 by Ronald F. Lazenby

All scripture quotations are taken from the King James Version of the Bible. Public domain.

Trilogy Christian Publishing/TBN and colophon are trademarks of Trinity Broadcasting Network.

Cover art by Ronald F. Lazenby

For information about special discounts for bulk purchases, please contact Trilogy Christian Publishing.

Trilogy Disclaimer: The views and content expressed in this book are those of the author and may not necessarily reflect the views and doctrine of Trilogy Christian Publishing or the Trinity Broadcasting Network.

Manufactured in the United States of America

10 9 8 7 6 5 4 3 2 1

Library of Congress Cataloging-in-Publication Data is available.

ISBN: 978-1-68556-008-9

E-ISBN: 978-1-68556-009-6

Dedicated to:

the Almighty One who gave me the ability to write this book

and

the sweetest and most loving daughter, son-in-law, and
granddaughter a man can have—
Tara, Grant, and Macy Lynne Woolwine.

# Table of Contents

# A FISHERMAN'S LIFE

*How much more death can I take?*

The dark clouds continue to produce bright flashes of lightning over the water as the fishing boats approach the shore of the Sea of Galilee. I am glad to be safely ashore but shaken by the heartbreaking news quickly spreading among the fishermen. During the storm, a twenty-year-old fisherman was swept overboard into the turbulent surf and drowned.

The distant rumbles of thunder are a constant reminder of the tragedy that occurred as if announcing the arrival of the boat containing the storm's victim. And the chill of the falling rain makes it even more miserable and difficult for me to complete the required tasks. Like the end of every day of fishing, the nets must be mended, washed, dried, and folded to prepare for the next day's work. Normally, the fishy smell of the nets does not bother me, but today the odor turns my stomach.

Suddenly the thunder ceases, and all is quiet. Grasping each corner of a folded net, four men exit one of the boats carrying the lifeless body of the sea's victim. The crowd of fishermen on land stand reverently on both sides for the procession to pass through its midst while the ones still on boats watch in silence. Following the Jewish custom among mourners to tear one's clothing, the distraught father of the victim has ripped his tunic from the neck to the waist. As he follows the corpse, he beats his chest in agony. I feel his pain. His continuous wails are excruciating to hear and remind me of my own loss. I muffle a sob.

As the procession passes by me, I am unable to hold back the tears and hope no one sees me as I brush them from my cheeks. But Abba does not miss much. Without looking or saying anything, he gives my shoulder a consoling squeeze as if he knows what I am thinking. Both my wife Arat and first-born child—a baby boy—died during

7

childbirth less than four months ago. That has consumed my thoughts ever since. The grief over my loss is unbearable, and the loneliness overwhelms me. Fishing daily helps fill the deep void their deaths left behind—until days like today. I just cannot cope with any more death.

However, I must not let that interfere with my responsibilities; I owe it to my family because they have been so supportive these past few months. I know it has been hard on them to watch me grieve as they are dealing with the deaths, too. Each time I have repeated the scenario of Arat's death, they have shown empathy and compassion— sharing tears and crying on each other's shoulders. They have tried to cheer me up by reminding me of the good times Arat and I had. I appreciate their actions and concerns, but I cannot seem to climb out of this deep dark hole.

It is expected of me to follow in my father's footsteps. Abba is a fisherman, so I have trained to be like him since I could walk. Or so it seems. I continue learning new things to improve my skills. I know where to look for schools of fish, how to cast a net from the shore or from a boat, which fish to keep and which to discard, and how to mend nets and sails. I can even salt and preserve fish so they will not spoil. For my age, I have the reputation among the local fishermen of being excellent at my trade.

But is being a fisherman how I want to spend the rest of my life?

My father Jesse and his brother Seba run the generations-old family fishing business from the shores of Bethsaida with the help of their uncle, Benjamin. I am Matthias, the only child of Jesse and Rachel. My best friend and younger cousin, Joseph, is the only child of my aunt Martha and uncle Seba. Soon it will be up to the two of us to continue the family business.

I look up from mending my net and watch Seba and Abba approach the hated Jewish tax collector's table and his Roman guard. I wonder how much the greedy publican will tax us today. How much of our hard-earned money will he pocket for himself?

My thoughts return to the life of a fisherman—or the death of one. "Joseph, that fisherman who washed overboard today could have been one of us. That thought scares me. I don't know if I can keep doing this."

Joseph stores his net and turns toward me. "I feel the same way and would love to do something different, Matthias. But what alternative do we have? Our family is a fishing family. We have been trained to be fishermen and are not skilled at any other profession."

Eyeing him sideways to see his reaction, I continue, "I have been thinking about that and have an idea if you are agreeable to it. We will have a somewhat different path, but first, we need to persuade our fathers. That may be the most difficult part since we will not be with them every day."

Joseph's eyes light up with obvious interest. "At this moment, it is not going to take much to persuade me. Let's hear your proposal."

I stop and lay the net down at my feet. I look directly at Joseph. "Here is my plan. What if you and I alternate going to the other villages and exchanging our fish for the items our family requires? We get the things we need by selling or trading the fish we have caught. Plus, we do not have to fish or work on the boat every day."

Joseph furrows his brow and scratches his head. "Benjamin is already trading the smoked fish for wood to repair the boats, flax for nets and sails, stones for anchors, baskets for fish, and grain for bread. What would we be doing?"

"The other day, I overheard him telling Abba that he needs to slow down because he is getting too old, his health is worsening, and soon he will not be able to make some of the longer trips. However, if he still wants to travel to the closer villages, he can continue to do that. We can go to the ones farther away."

"I like your idea. When do you want to surprise our fathers with it? Should we tell them together or separately?"

"Let us practice what we want to say and tell them together.

What about tomorrow?"

Tonight, the nightmares are even worse than usual. When I drift off to sleep, I relive the death of my wife and son. I hear Arat's painful cries as she tries to deliver my already dead son. I hear my mother holler, "Matthias, come quick! The bleeding will not stop. Arat needs you!" I rush into the room, see Arat soaked in blood, and gag as the chord is being cut from around the neck of the dead baby. I lean over Arat's pale, colorless face as she weakly whispers, "I'm sorry, Matthias," before her eyes glaze over into the deadly stare. I scream "NOOO!" and wake up sobbing.

Mother lightly rubs my shoulder and lays beside me. "Another nightmare, son?"

"Yes, the same one as usual."

She puts her arm around me, and I fall back asleep. But in addition to the recurring nightmares of seeing the dead faces of my wife and son, I keep having repeating dreams of being hit by a wave and thrown into the turbulent surf—drowning like the young fisherman earlier today. I wake up several times gasping for air and soaking in sweat.

Daylight is a welcome relief from my restless night. To be in the warm sunshine and see the glistening ripples of the water as we net fish from the shore helps to lift the darkness that is overshadowing my thoughts.

After several hours of fishing, the four of us stop for a break. Joseph and I hurriedly eat our smoked fish and bread in the shade of a nearby tree while Abba and Seba sit on a couple of large rocks next to the shore. We have been anxious to tell our fathers of our plans but just have not worked up enough nerve or had the right opportunity... until now.

"Joseph, it is now or never. Let's go tell them." I grab Joseph's hand to pull him to his feet. My palms are so sweaty he almost falls, causing us to both laugh. At least that breaks the tension. A little.

Abba notices our hesitation in walking toward our fathers. "You two look troubled. What is wrong, boys?"

Trying to sound as mature and calm as possible, I answer with a shaky voice, "We have something important to discuss with both of you."

Seba looks at Abba. "This does not sound good, Jesse." He turns his attention back to us. "Have a seat, boys. What's bothering you?"

Obeying him, we sit down. I begin by admitting I am being selfish by what we are proposing and thank them for their understanding and compassion for me since Arat's and the baby's death. "I am not handling their deaths well, as you already know. And after the death of the fisherman yesterday...." I gulp. "His death scared me. I don't know if I can commit to fishing from the boat for the rest of my life."

Abba reaches over and squeezes my hand. "I understand your pain, son."

While we present our idea, our fathers lean toward us as if it will make them hear better. When we conclude, Seba rests his chin on his hand. "I don't know, boys. We will be losing at least one fisherman every time one of you is gone. Those of us fishing will have to work even harder than we already do. I do not see how we can do that. Our families will suffer if we lose a fisherman."

Abba strokes his beard and looks at Seba. "But just a few days ago, Benjamin did say he can't continue making the long journeys into the villages to sell or trade our fish for the things we need. We need someone to replace him—at least for the longer trips. Once they are trained, we would have one of them here to fish while the other is gone. I know Benjamin is not as strong and agile as the boys, but maybe he could fish when the boys are gone, and the boys could still fish with us when they are both home. At least Benjamin's replacement would be a member of our family."

Abba and Seba talk among themselves before Abba stands. "We can try it for a short while and see how it works, and hopefully, it will work out. If it does not, we will adjust. Tomorrow, Benjamin is supposed to meet us at the boat before we go out fishing. Let us see what he thinks."

Seba grabs his net. "I imagine he will be happy to teach you boys his part of the trade. Although you are not going to be danger-free on your journeys, you will be safer than being on the boat every day."

Abba puts his arm around my shoulder and looks into my eyes. "When anyone loses his or her life at such a young age like the young man yesterday...or Arat, it makes us all stop and realize how our lives can be snatched from us at any moment. That is the main reason we are casting from the shore today."

With my eyes clouded by tears, all I can say is, "I know."

He smiles and pats me on the back. "For now, we need to return to fishing."

That went far better than I expected.

Joseph and I do not want to scare any fish close to shore, so we sneak into the shallow water while Abba and Seba are casting their nets a little farther up the shoreline. Once we toss our circular nets, I glance over at Joseph and whisper, "What do you think Benjamin's response will be?"

# AN ALTERNATIVE

The next morning while Joseph and I are ensuring the weights and floats of the dragnets are properly secured for a day of boat-fishing, we see Benjamin slowly hobbling toward our fathers. On a fishing excursion several years ago, he suffered a broken leg which did not heal properly. This morning not only is he barely picking up his foot, but he is dragging it as if it is weighted down and it is taking every ounce of energy to move it. He is even using a walking stick. He does not do that often. Having been in the fishing business all his life has taken its toll on him.

"Shalom," Abba greets him with a hug. "Do you want to go fishing with us today, Benjamin?"

"I wish I could schedule some fishing into my day. It looks like we are going to have nice weather today. However, I need to run some errands and get some things done around here before I head south tomorrow on another one of those long, dreaded trips." That is typical Benjamin. Knowing the work must be done regardless of how he feels, he always pushes himself to complete the needed tasks. I admire that about him.

Abba takes advantage of Benjamin's statement to introduce our proposition. "We need to talk to you about that, Benjamin. Our sons have a proposal for you I think you are going to like." Abba motions for us to join them and pats me on the shoulder. "Our sons have an idea which could be the solution to your problems."

After hearing our plan and the reason behind it, Benjamin winks at Joseph and me accompanied with a huge smile. "Boys, the way I feel this morning, you are welcome to take over this job anytime you want. The sooner, the better." Benjamin looks at Abba and Seba. "In fact, they are welcome to go with me tomorrow if you approve. I have some deliveries to make over the next several days and can use the extra muscle. It will give them a sample of what will be expected of them."

13

Joseph and I clasp each other's shoulders and shake one another as our fathers give their approval. "I admit it is short notice, but you might as well start training immediately. We will miss having you boys with us every day." Abba has a tear in his eye and gives me a hug. "But you will not be gone long and can always fish with us when you get home."

While the three of them handle the business for which Benjamin initially came, Joseph and I continue preparing the boat for a day of fishing. "We have a long journey, so I will see you boys at dawn." Benjamin waves to us as he shuffles away. He seems to have a little more pep in his step now and is no longer using the stick for support.

"We will be there, bright and early!" I exclaim as we both return the wave.

The next morning as Joseph and I cross the common courtyard separating all our homes, Benjamin has already loaded the wagon with all the baskets of smoked fish we are trading. I tote a bundle of fruits and raw vegetables and a basket of smoked fish and bread to the wagon. "I hope there is room in the wagon for this food Mother prepared."

"We do not have a lot of room, but we will make room for that." Benjamin laughs and rubs his stomach. "And I am impressed by your punctuality, too. You boys are off to a good start. Are you ready to leave?"

"Anytime you are. I laid awake most of last night thinking about our venture. When I am not having nightmares, laying awake at night is nothing new since Arat and my son died. I hope being off the boat and away from Bethsaida will help break that habit. I am really looking forward to a change."

"I am glad you are excited, Matthias. The excitement may wear off over time as things become more routine. But almost every trip has at least one unexpected challenge. An anticipated trade does not occur, or a caravan is either too slow or too fast. You encounter bad weather or problems with people at campsites. Those things are what makes life interesting, though. I think you boys are going to enjoy this job—I know I have. I wish I could continue making these long trips, but I just cannot keep up the pace that I used to." Benjamin grimaces at the thought.

Benjamin waves goodbye to his wife Elizabeth, who has been standing in the doorway of their home and watching us. Although Benjamin is moving a little quicker this morning, I help him climb onto the wagon. "Sorry, but only two of us can ride in the wagon at a time with the load we are carrying right now." He points to the donkey. "We don't want to kill Old Job here, so you will need to take turns riding in the wagon. You two need to decide who gets to ride first."

I quickly hop on the seat beside Benjamin and turn toward Joseph. "Looks like you are going to be walking for a while."

Joseph grins broadly. "I do not have a problem with that. It is cool right now. But it will be a lot warmer in the heat of the day while you are walking on the hot, dusty path, and I am relaxing up there in the wagon."

Although I laugh, it is true. It will be hotter when I am walking. "Where are we going?"

"Jericho. It is known for its pottery and baskets. You have some cousins there who are the best in the business. And do not let the distance scare you. I only go there every couple of months to trade fish. Since this trip is one of the longest trips I make, it will be an excellent learning experience for you two."

We follow the coastline down the eastern coast of the Sea of Galilee, stopping in Gergesa and Hippos to trade our fish for supplies. We stay on the eastern shore of the Jordan River through Perea to avoid defilement by contact with Samaritans. We set up camp and bathe in the river while the sun is still high enough to warm us. After eating some of the food Mother prepared, we settle down by the fire to sleep—at least Benjamin and Joseph sleep. I keep prodding the fire until late in the night before I can finally doze.

For safety reasons, we travel in caravans as much as possible, but since we are slowed down by our heavy load, we change caravans daily as we make the long trek to Jericho. Benjamin talks almost constantly, trying to tell us everything he can recall about our new duties and introduces us to many of his contacts in the villages we visit. Along the way, we trade some of our fish for fruit, bread, vegetables, and even provisions for Old Job.

After several days, we enter the walls of Jericho just before the sun sets. Since Jericho is one of the oldest cities and caters to the wealthiest people, beggars are numerous and approach us immediately asking for food. They are thankful for the few fish we toss them.

Benjamin steers Old Job down the city street, and we soon arrive at our cousins' home—actually, it is my aunt and uncle's home. Although it has been a while since I last saw them, I recognize them immediately. Hannah, my mother's sister, hugs me tightly while her two daughters, Deborah and Chava, stand shyly in the doorway. When we enter the home, we are greeted by her husband, Gershom, and three sons, Moshe, Samuel, and Lemuel.

Hannah brings a tray of bread, olives, and cheese for us to snack on while she and the girls finish preparing the meal. "After several days on the road, you need a home-cooked meal. Sit down and eat. You must be hungry."

And she was correct. I fill up on a meal of challah, lentils, figs, latkes, and chicken. I am stuffed.

Although Hannah is a few years older than my mother and beginning to get gray streaks in her hair, there is a close resemblance. They have the same facial features and even similar facial expressions. Hannah is a little heavier than Mother, but they are the same height. When I tell her about the death of Arat and the baby, she even cries like Mother.

Although tired and with stomachs still full, we all sit outside and talk well into the night...until we are too sleepy to talk anymore. Joseph and I follow Moshe, Samuel, and Lemuel up the wooden ladder to the flat roof. Because it is a clear night and the temperature is so pleasant, we decide to sleep there instead of inside the house. We chat for a few minutes, but they are soon sound asleep.

I listen to their rhythmic breathing and gaze at the twinkling stars and the full moon, but sleep will not come. I begin counting the stars until my eyelids are too heavy to keep open. I wake startled. My body is covered in sweat. Another nightmare. Closing my eyes, all I see is the cold and dead faces of Arat and the baby. We did not even get a chance to name him. "God, I can't continue to live like this. Help me find peace."

I begin counting the stars again. When my eyes close, there are the faces, again. I quickly open my eyes and start counting again...one, two, three. The last number I remember is seven hundred and eleven.

I am awakened by the rooster crowing at dawn. As the sun creeps above the horizon, we exchange our fish for some clay water pots and newly woven baskets to store and haul fish. With the wagon loaded, we bid our relatives farewell and begin the journey home. This time, the three of us can all comfortably ride in the wagon together since we have a lighter load for Old Job to haul.

Benjamin often repeats himself as he continues to tell us about his experiences—both good and bad. He warns us this route up the western shore of the Jordan River toward Samaria is more prone to thieves, so we join a caravan before we even exit the city walls.

"If you do not remember anything else I tell you, remember this bit of advice because it could save your lives. Take if from a voice of experience—there is safety in numbers."

"I do not take this route if I can avoid it when I am alone, but since there are three of us and we can keep up the pace of this caravan, I feel safe. Many years ago, I had heard rumors this route was dangerous and always joined caravans, but I had never encountered any problems. Until one time, I got separated from the caravan I was with—I could not keep up their pace and told them to go ahead. I did not want to slow them down, so I was left traveling alone." He points toward some rocks. "This is the exact spot—from behind both sides of those rocks was a band of eight robbers. I tried to fight back, but there were too many of them. They surrounded me and took everything—my wagon and mule, the pottery and baskets, my provisions, including my clothes. They roughed me up and left me on the side of the road, but at least they did not take my life. Luckily, there was a caravan about two hours behind me who took care of me and carried me back to Bethsaida. If it had not been for them, I might not be here today."

I pat Benjamin on the back. "We are glad you are here."

He smiles. "So just remember...travel with a caravan when taking this road. Never travel this way alone. And never stray off the path."

# THE BAPTISM

By the ninth hour, we approach what looks like a city of tents littering the banks of the Jordan River. Benjamin begins pointing out good areas to camp and areas to avoid. "You will encounter some odd people and see some strange things at some of these camp sites." The smell of fish being cooked over the crackling flames is welcoming. But the laughter of children playing is a reminder I will never get to hear my son laugh. I cannot let that thought linger—I need to shift my focus to something else.

Benjamin points. "That looks like a good spot."

He steers Old Job toward an open area next to where two burly men are waving at him. He returns their waves. "You may know these men since they are both fishermen from Bethsaida."

"It would be nice to see some familiar faces because I am feeling a little homesick." I shade my eyes from the afternoon sun to examine them more closely.

Do I recognize them? They do seem vaguely familiar. Obviously, they are brothers. Although there is some age difference, they have the same weathered facial features, curly hair, and broad shoulders. A loud booming voice greets Benjamin. "Shalom. It has been a long time since we last saw you."

"It's good to see you, Simon...and you too, Andrew," Benjamin gives each of the two brothers a hug and kiss on the cheek. "This is Joseph and Matthias, my nephews' sons. If all goes as planned, they are going to be assuming my duties, especially on these longer trips. They are from Bethsaida, so you may already know each other."

"You are Seba's and Jesse's sons, aren't you? You may not remember us, but we remember you." Andrew laughs as he recollects the night. "We were on the boat the first time you went night fishing. You boys did not handle the storm very well, but that is what makes it so memorable. I felt sorry for you boys because I don't think I have ever seen anyone as seasick as you two were."

I feel the blood rushing to my face. "All I remember is 'feeding the fish.' But now I am accustomed to fishing from the boat."

"Yes, but you still 'feed the fish' on a regular basis." Joseph punches me in the arm as everyone laughs.

Benjamin becomes more serious. "You boys tie up Old Job and go roaming around if you like. I want to hear more about this fellow Andrew and Simon have been spending so much time with lately." He points to a short, stocky, wild-looking man dressed in a camel-hair coat with long matted hair and scraggly beard. "He is a strange-looking character, and I've heard some stories about him."

"I am a little curious who he is, too, and why are all those people listening so intently to him?" Joseph stares at the man surrounded by a large group of people. "I would not want to meet him on a deserted road. He's scary looking."

Simon leans toward Joseph, but even his whisper is loud enough for all of us to hear. "He is peculiar, but he is nothing to be afraid of. He is an excellent teacher and says he is a 'messenger of God' to tell us the Messiah is coming very soon. Some think he is a great prophet, and some even believe he is the Messiah himself, but he declares he is not."

"And some just think he is a lunatic." I laugh, but my joke does not go over well. I am the only one who thinks it is funny because I receive dirty looks from Simon, Andrew, and especially Benjamin.

Andrew glares at me. "Some do, Matthias, but we believe him. That 'lunatic' is John the Baptist, and he has many followers who have confessed their sins and been baptized. In fact, he is about to baptize someone now." He points as another man is led into the river. The calm water ripples around their feet as they enter.

A hush falls over the crowd, and we all stop and stare. There is something about the man being led into the water which draws everyone's attention to him, including the children. I do not know exactly what it is. All I do know is I, along with everyone else, am mesmerized by him and cannot stop watching him. He has Jewish facial features and skin tone but has lighter-colored hair and eyes than most Jews. His hair and beard are long but neatly trimmed. He is tall, thin, and muscular, but he has a gentle, meek demeanor. He is the exact opposite of the wild-looking man leading him into the water.

John the Baptist begins speaking to the crowd, and we all listen intently. "This is the One I have been telling you is coming who will baptize you with the Holy Ghost and with fire." He shifts his focus to the man about to be baptized. "He is the One you should follow. I need to be baptized by You, and You come to me?"

Is he saying this man is our Messiah?

After the man is baptized, I stand frozen in shock as He comes up out of the river. A dove descends and lights upon the man's shoulder, looks at the Man's face, and catches a drop of water from His beard before flying away. I look around to see who is speaking when I hear a deep voice echo from the sky. "This is my beloved Son, in whom I am well pleased."

Who was that? Where did that come from? Am I imagining all this? Do I dare ask anyone if they saw and heard what I did? If they did not, they would think I have lost my mind, and I am not sure I have not. What just happened?

The Man and John the Baptist share a warm embrace when they exit the river, and the Man disappears into the crowd. I am relieved when suddenly everyone in the crowd starts talking about the unusual events we all witnessed. As the level of excitement and conversation increases, the Man is nowhere to be seen.

"John, where did that Man go?" someone calls out. "Who is He?"

The Baptist replies, "I am only the messenger announcing the arrival of the Lamb of God who takes away the sin of the world. Where He goes, I do not know."

When the man does not reappear, many in the crowd wander off trying to find Him, while others remain by the river bewildered. Since nightfall is approaching, we spread our cloaks beside Simon's and Andrew's and build a campfire as the sun sets over the Jordan River. We share a meal of figs and bread Hannah packed for us and fish cooked over the open fire the two brothers caught earlier in the day.

By now, I am convinced we have all experienced something extraordinary. Is He really the Messiah we have been waiting for, like the wild-looking man said? Benjamin looks at Simon and Andrew. "I know the two of you have been with John the Baptist for a while. What are your plans now since the man he proclaims as the Messiah has come?"

"Since the One we have been waiting for has disappeared, I think I will go do some fishing with Father." Simon looks at Andrew to see what his plans are.

Andrew agrees with his brother and completes the sentence. "And we will follow the Messiah when He returns."

I lay back on my cloak. "I've never seen or heard anything like that before. And I would certainly like to know more about Him. Who is He? I was hypnotized by Him, and I don't know why."

"Me, too," Joseph prods the fire with a stick. "I don't know if He really is the Messiah we have been taught about all our lives, but what just occurred sure makes me wonder."

Benjamin watches the cloud of ashes as they fly into the air and then lays down. "We've all shared something today that could change our lives forever. If He is who John says, and He very well could be, today is only the beginning of many great changes to come for our people."

The next morning, while a few of the followers of John the Baptist choose to stay with him beside the Jordan River, many are packing their supplies and leaving. Simon, Andrew, and several other followers join our caravan. They are all noticeably quiet except for an occasional comment contemplating what their next move will be. Some say they are unsure of their decision to leave John the Baptist and are wondering if they are making the right choice. Others say they will follow the Messiah whenever He is found. Some are choosing to return to their homes to resume "normal" lives. Unlike most in the caravan, Simon and Andrew have not wavered from their decision. Simon, the more vocal of the two brothers, declares his intentions where everyone can hear. "I will follow the Messiah."

When we eventually reach the outskirts of Bethsaida, the brothers say their good-byes and head toward their father's house. Soon after, we arrive at our family compound, and our fathers are standing there smiling. "How did you know we were going to be home today?" I jump down and run to Abba.

"Just a lucky guess," Abba greets me with a tight embrace and a kiss on the cheek.

By this time, Joseph has jumped down and is hugging Seba. "Don't let him fool you. He has been moping around here for the last two days. He has really been missing you, Matthias."

"And I have missed you, too, Abba." I give him a tight squeeze.

Benjamin pulls Elizabeth tightly to him as she comes out the door to where we are standing. "It is nice to be home again."

With a big grin, Joseph looks at his father. "Yes, as nice as it was to get away, I am glad to be home, too."

"You have a lot to tell us. How was the trip, boys?" Seba winks at Joseph.

Before we can respond, Benjamin puts his arms around Joseph's and my shoulders. "You ought to be proud of these two. They are quick learners." He continues to tell our fathers about our accomplishments and the many business contacts we met, and of course, brought them up to date on the friends and relatives we had encountered.

"When we camped by the Jordan River, we even met Simon and Andrew, a couple of fishermen from here. They even remembered us from our first night-fishing trip."

I regret making that statement as soon as the words exit my mouth. Abba and Seba cannot stop laughing. Finally, Seba catches his breath. "You boys made that a memorable night for everyone that was aboard that boat."

"I guess that night will always haunt us, Matthias. At least, I have outgrown it but can't say the same for you." We all laugh again.

Benjamin becomes serious. "Yes, Simon and Andrew have been following John the Baptist for a while. I know you have heard rumors about him. And he is as strange-looking as the rumors say."

"Oh, yes, we have. He is the one who many think is the Messiah, isn't he?"

Abba quickly shifts his gaze to me when I respond to his comment. "He does not claim to be the Messiah, only the one introducing Him. And we think we saw the Messiah, too."

"Don't you boys be deceived by him too easily. You know there are a lot of men out there claiming to be the Messiah."

Joseph quickly comes to my defense. "I don't mean to be disrespectful, but you do not understand what we experienced. John the Baptist introduced this man being baptized as the Messiah. After the baptism, a dove came down and lit on this man's shoulder as He was coming up from the water. Then, a voice from out of nowhere said, 'This is my beloved Son,' and the Messiah vanished into the crowd. No one knows where He went. It was amazing!"

"I was there, too," Benjamin gives my shoulder a supportive squeeze. "What we all saw and heard was very persuasive, and although I am not totally convinced, He could be the real thing. He will not have to do too much more for me to believe He is the Messiah."

"Me, too," Joseph and I say in unison.

"Be very careful, boys...and you too, Benjamin!" Abba looks disappointed and sternly warns. "The three of you sound like you are already hooked. As much as I would like for the Messiah to come and deliver us from the hands of the Romans, all I will say is, keep your eyes and ears open. Don't take the bait too quickly."

"Abba, I definitely want to see more of Him before I decide for sure. But what we saw was not natural. There was something extraordinary and captivating about Him."

"Given the chance, we need to check out this man for ourselves, Seba. These three have certainly seen something which impressed them. Hopefully, they are right, and this man is our Messiah."

# WALKING AWAY

Nearly six weeks have passed since Joseph and I assumed a portion of Benjamin's role in the family business. Benjamin continues to provide tips as he accompanies us on short trips, as well as introducing us to key business associates. We not only consider him a business associate but also look at him as a "father figure" when he is with us. It is a pleasure having him along on our jaunts, if only for fatherly advice.

Everywhere we go, we hear the man we saw baptized is in Galilee preaching that "the time is fulfilled" and "the kingdom of God is at hand," but we have not seen Him since the baptism. Although the memory of His baptism remains imbedded in my mind, some have identified Him as Jesus of Nazareth, the son of Joseph, a carpenter. That does not sound too impressive to me. Can anything good come from Nazareth? Would our Messiah be the son of a carpenter? I know what I saw and heard, but I am not sure what to believe anymore. I guess time will reveal His true identity. At least, I hope it does.

While we are at home, Joseph and I go fishing with our fathers. Even Benjamin is tagging along on some of our recent fishing excursions, including this current one. We have been at sea the last two nights, and it has been a successful fishing trip. It will be nice to be back on solid ground for a few days. I do still get a little sick from the boat swaying to and fro, but I cannot tell anyone—they will never stop kidding me.

By the time we sort and count our catch, it is nearly noon. We have a large haul of fish to smoke and preserve...and pay taxes on. As we get off the boat for Abba and Seba to go pay the dishonest and corrupt tax collector, a large group of fishermen from the largest fishing cooperative in the area owned by Zebedee and Jona are standing on the dock. An angry voice bellows out. "What do you mean the man asked them to follow him, and they just stopped what they were doing and walked away?"

"I am sorry, Zeb, but that is exactly what happened."

"Why didn't you stop them? That is just not like James and John. Who was this man anyway?"

"I don't know, but the same thing happened with Simon and Andrew, too. They immediately threw down their nets and followed him." Abba identifies the voice of Jona, the father of Simon and Andrew.

Zeb inquires about where they went, and I guess someone pointed in our direction because the entire group of fishermen heads toward us. Seba is the first to say anything to Zebedee, the enraged father of James and John. "What happened, Zeb?"

The group of men stops, and Zebedee responds more calmly, yet frustration can be detected in his voice. "A man came and asked them to follow him, and our sons," pointing to Jona and himself, "merely left with him without saying a word to anyone. I do not understand. It is not like my sons to do something that irresponsible."

Benjamin eyes the group and asks if anyone knew this man or what he looked like. Several fishermen respond.

"He was a stranger—probably in his late twenties or early thirties."

"Although he looked Jewish, the color of his hair and eyes were lighter than ours."

"And He spoke gently, but with conviction when He told them to follow Him."

"He was unusual looking—different than anyone I have ever seen."

Benjamin, Joseph, and I exchange glances, knowing exactly who they are describing. "It is the Messiah." I must have whispered my thoughts to Joseph more loudly than I thought because Zebedee approaches me. He is almost a head taller and much larger than I am. With a beet-red face and nostrils flared, his face is only a few inches from mine. A vein in his forehead pulses and looks like it is going to explode. "You know him! Who is he?"

Benjamin comes to my defense as I take a step back. "Calm down, Zeb. The description these men have given fits the Man we saw John the Baptist baptized in the River Jordan." I stand there quietly and too afraid to speak or move.

Still angry, Zebedee turns back toward me. "Well, where are they?"

This time Abba steps in between Zebedee and me, glaring at him. Abba's feet are planted far apart, his chest is thrust out, and his arms are away from his body. His hands are clenched into tight fists. Now he is the one with the beet-red face and bulging vein in his forehead. Is he going to punch Zebedee?

"You will have to ask your sons that question because my son has been with me on the boat for the past two nights." They continue to stare into each other's eyes and not flinch.

Apparently, Simon and Andrew have been telling their father about the baptism. "Is he the man some think is the Messiah?"

Benjamin nods but does not take his eyes off Abba and Zebedee. "Yes, He's the One."

"Then that explains Simon's and Andrew's reaction." Jona seems to be reassured. "They have been waiting for Him to reappear and did not know where to find Him. I guess He found them instead."

Jona tries to ease the tension and pats Zebedee on the shoulder. "Come on, Zeb. They do not know where our boys are. They will show up eventually."

Zebedee continues to glare at my father as he backs away but offers no apology for his actions. Abba turns and begins to walk away. "Come on, fellows. We have a lot to do before we can go home. It has been a long two days—too long to worry about the missing fishermen."

Zebedee mumbles something under his breath, but Abba ignores him. Our fathers lead us to the boat. When we get far enough away from him, I whisper to Joseph. "I do not know if I could leave Abba and Seba at the spur of the moment to follow the possible Messiah like they did. But I want to be a part of it if He is the Messiah."

Benjamin overhears me and winks. "Me, too, Matthias. Maybe we can incorporate some of our trips around His ministry."

Joseph and I acknowledge Benjamin's comment with a mischievous smile while the group of fishermen continues their conversation about the whereabouts of the four missing fishermen.

"Thank you, Abba, for stepping in back there. And you, too, Benjamin."

"That man has such a quick temper, but he is harmless. It is out-of-character for his sons to wander away, and he is just worried about them. You were the easiest target for him to take his frustration on. But I could not just stand there and let him do it." Abba puts his arm around my shoulder and laughs. "I have to protect my baby boy when he is in danger."

By the time we unload the fish and clean and mend the nets, Zebedee, Jona, and the other fishermen are nowhere in sight.

As time passes, rumors run rampant throughout Bethsaida. Philip, another local fisherman, and his friend, Nathaniel, are said to have joined the group following the Messiah. Simon and Andrew have been seen at their homes in Capernaum, where Simon's mother-in-law is said to be deathly ill. It is even rumored that the Messiah is also living in Capernaum since he has brothers there.

Since our last fishing expedition was so successful, and we have all the fish counted, smoked, and ready to trade, Benjamin decides a trip to a more inland village like Cana is in order. We will be passing through Capernaum on our return trip to conduct some business. In reality, we hope the trip will give us the opportunity to possibly witness the Messiah performing these so-called miracles we have been hearing about or at least dispel some rumors.

# PROVEN RUMORS

Arriving in Cana, I recount last night's discussion between my mother and father. "Mother had her back turned to us while she was cooking and said she simply could not understand why all these men are dropping what they are doing and leaving their families to follow a man claiming to be the Messiah without any proof whatsoever. Before I could even offer an explanation, Abba held up his hand for me to be quiet, and without saying we were the ones who told him, he told her what we saw. I think he knows we would consider joining the group following the Messiah if given the right opportunity. She didn't really say much except 'the story' was intriguing, and these men should be more responsible and not be leaving their families in a bind just to see if He is the real thing."

"We are all curious about who this man is, including both of your fathers. On our fishing trip, both asked me several times to describe what we saw and heard and what I thought about Him. Now, they are afraid you will follow Him without any warning like Simon, Andrew, James, and John. Plus, I think they suspect we have an ulterior motive for taking this trip and secretly hope we return home with some decisive information."

Joseph chuckles. "They didn't ask very many questions about why we are taking this trip, did they?"

We conduct our business and spend the night in Cana. If we thought there were a lot of rumors floating around Bethsaida, it is no comparison to the scores of rumors circulating in Cana. Everyone is still talking about the "social event of the season"—the huge wedding festivities which occurred last week, who and where the guests were from, not to mention the finest wine ever served in the area.

The rumors claim due to the large number of guests and poor planning on his part, the bridegroom ran out of wine in mid-week of the seven-day wedding festivities. Jesus of Nazareth happened to be attending this wedding. When He found out that the bridegroom had run out of wine, He asked the servants to fill six waterpots with water, then somehow changed that water to "the best wine anyone had ever tasted." After the wedding, Jesus, His family, and those with Him returned to Capernaum. How could a normal man do that?

After some calculations, I reveal my results, "Yes, changing water into wine is a miracle itself, but six water pots. That is approximately one-hundred twenty to one-hundred eighty gallons if each water pot holds twenty to thirty gallons. That is a lot of wine!"

"I bet the guests did enjoy the festivities. With that much wine, I am surprised anyone even remembers the wedding." We all laugh at Joseph's comment.

On our way to Capernaum, we stop at the market in Gennesaret to buy flax to replace our ship's weathered sails. We hear footsteps approaching as we finish loading the wagon. "What brings you fellows to Gennesaret?"

We turn and see Andrew walking toward us. "Shalom. The boys and I are here mainly to find you, Simon, and the Messiah and determine if the rumors we have heard are true. Plus, doing a little business."

"You would not believe what Simon and I have seen since we started following Jesus."

"Turning water into wine sounds pretty impressive to me. What really happened?"

"You have heard about that already? News travels fast, and that is only the beginning, Matthias. I do not know what you have heard, but if I had not been there and seen it personally, I would not have believed it myself."

Andrew leads us to a place where we can sit in the shade of a tree while he continues to recall the event. "I do not think Mary, the mother of Jesus, had any idea what was about to occur when she called for Him and us to come to the wedding."

"The third day of the marriage ceremony, Mary discovered there was no more wine and told Jesus. I still do not understand the meaning of His response because He called her 'woman' and said His 'time was not yet come,' but she did not seem offended by it. She told the servants to do whatever He said to do. He looked skyward and said a prayer, then pointed to six water pots and told the servants to fill the jars to the brim with water. When the jars were full, He told them to draw some out and take it to the chief steward. We all looked at Him like He was crazy—why should they take water to the chief steward when he is expecting wine. However, they did what Jesus said. The water miraculously became wine, and when the steward tasted it, he asked the bridegroom why he was saving the best wine until the last. I know it sounds unbelievable, but I witnessed it myself."

I shoot a glance at Benjamin's and Joseph's dumbfounded faces. "Yes, it is unbelievable."

"And it was the best wine I have ever tasted. When we left the wedding, we returned to Capernaum. Since His brothers live there, Jesus has made Capernaum His home base for His ministry."

"So, the rumor is true. By the way, we heard Simon's mother-in-law is extremely ill. How is she doing?"

"Funny you should mention that, Benjamin, because that is another miracle. Last Sabbath after Jesus removed an unclean spirit from a man at the synagogue...."

"Whoa! We have not heard about this, Andrew. What happened?"

"Like I said earlier, Matthias, you will not believe what all we have seen. Jesus even has power over demons!" He pauses to let his statement sink in. "After He had finished teaching in the synagogue, there was a man with an unclean spirit who cried out asking Jesus if He had come to destroy them and calling Him 'the Holy One of God.' Jesus rebuked the demon, and it immediately came out of the man."

Benjamin, Joseph, and I exchange looks but remain silent, leaning in closer to hear what Andrew will tell us next. He takes a deep breath. "We returned to Simon's house after we left the synagogue and found the fever of his mother-in-law was worse. She was near death and unresponsive. Jesus stood over her, took her hand, and told the fever to come out of her. Immediately the fever left her, her strength returned, and she stood and started ministering to us. Word spread throughout the city that afternoon, and by evening, people started bringing their sick family and friends to the house. Jesus healed them all regardless of whatever ailed them."

"He can change water to wine, drive out demons, and heal the sick. Is He our Messiah, Andrew?"

"I believe He is, Benjamin. In addition to all the miracles I have witnessed, He teaches with more authority, knowledge, and personal insight than any priest I have ever heard. And people are magically drawn to Him and follow Him wherever He goes."

Unless Andrew is exaggerating, I can't wait any longer. "I want to meet Him, Andrew. Where can I find Him?" Benjamin and Joseph insist they meet Him, too.

"You are in luck because He rose early the day after the Sabbath and went to be alone and pray. Some of His disciples, including Simon and me, followed Him here to Gennesaret. Maybe your paths will cross soon. By the way, we have been fishing here the last couple of days and could use some extra hands on a fishing trip tonight if you want to stay in the area for another day or two...and who knows, maybe you will get to meet Jesus while you are here."

It is too late in the day to travel home, so we follow Andrew to the dock where Simon is alone on the boat, making the final preparations to go night fishing. He is so preoccupied he does not notice us. "I found us some extra hands to go fishing tonight, Simon."

Simon grabs Joseph and me and laughs. "I hope it is not a stormy night like the last time we fished with you boys."

# UNUSUAL CATCH

Simon is apologetic as we all sit on the shore cleaning the nets. "Sorry, men. We did not even catch one fish the whole night. That was a waste of time."

Benjamin pats him on the back. "It was not a total waste. We enjoyed the camaraderie, Simon. And there is no need to apologize. We all know you can never predict what the fish will do."

"Plus, we enjoyed hearing the stories of your experiences with Jesus." I stifle a yawn. "The one you have not told is when Jesus told you to follow Him. Why didn't you tell your father you were leaving instead of walking away? He did not seem too disturbed once he knew who you left with, but James' and John's father was extremely upset." I tell them about our confrontation.

"James and John are not known for being the 'sons of thunder' for nothing." Andrew laughs. "He has quite a temper."

Simon then responds directly to my question, "Matthias, we did not mean to be disrespectful to our father, but we did not even think about it. We had been waiting for Jesus' return, and when He spoke and said to follow Him, we simply obeyed."

I blurt out my thought without thinking. "I don't think I could do that to my father."

Simon and Andrew sit silently with heads down and staring blankly at the ground as if my comment is the first time they have even considered the impact their actions may have had upon their father. "Jona understands how important finding the Messiah is to you and all Israel," Benjamin reassures them. "We all want to follow Him."

"Yes, we do." I stretch and yawn. "I hope we are able to see Him soon."

"Looks like you are going to get that opportunity." Andrew points to a large group of people heading our way. Even though I have only seen Him one time, I recognize the man leading the group as the one baptized by John the Baptist.

Joseph and I excitedly jump to our feet and assist Benjamin to his. We are joined by fishermen from other boats as we walk to meet Jesus. After Simon introduces us to James and John, he chuckles. "These boys have already met your father, especially Matthias."

James raises his eyebrows and scratches his beard. "Uh, oh. It sounds like there is more to this story. Our father reacts to things without thinking sometimes—lots of times. I hope he was not too rough on you."

I shrug my shoulders. "He was frustrated and did not know why you would walk away from your responsibilities to follow a stranger, especially without saying anything to anyone." I want to tell him how unpleasant the experience was for me but decide not to.

I do not know if he sees my discomfort or what, but John changes the subject. "I hope you fellows caught more fish than we did last night. I do not know where they were, but they were not in our nets. We did not catch even one."

"Neither did we," Andrew still sounds disappointed. "I thought conditions were right yesterday for a good night of fishing, but I guess I was wrong."

The crowd follows Jesus to the shoreline and complies when He tells them to be patient and stay onshore. He turns toward Simon. "Thrust the boat out from the land, so I can teach the people from your ship."

With a wink, Simon motions for Benjamin, Joseph, and me to join him. "Come on, fellows. I need some help here."

Jesus smiles at me as I help Him into the boat and His teeth are snow white. His eyes are even more unusual than I remember, too. Instead of being dark brown like most Jews, His are pale brown and almost clear and contrast with His dark complexion. His shoulder-length hair and beard have a golden tint to them and glistens in the sunlight. I remember him being tall, but He is even taller than I thought.

When He sits, we push the boat away from the shore and hurriedly jump onboard behind Him. The boat comes to a stop several feet from the shore, and Jesus begins to speak in a calm, soothing voice to the crowd, yet powerful enough, so the crowd is attentive and remains speechless. It is amazing that those in the back of the crowd seem to have no trouble hearing Jesus even though He is not shouting but talking in a normal tone.

Jesus speaks with the wisdom of the scribes, but His teachings seem more heartfelt than memorized. He emphasizes the public ceremonial rites performed by the scribes comply with the Law, but they should be a meaningful personal experience to the individual. Of course, Benjamin, Joseph, and I listen intently to every word Jesus says and look at each other when He concludes by declaring that "the prophecies in the scripture are this day being fulfilled." He is claiming to be our Messiah.

He finishes addressing the crowd and turns toward Simon, "Launch out into deeper water and let down your nets for a catch."

Simon does not look too happy with the idea of going fishing so soon after our disappointing night, and for that matter, neither am I. We had just finished cleaning the nets, and now we are going to throw them back into the water. "Master, we have toiled all night and caught nothing."

Looking at Jesus through tired and sleepy eyes, he shakes his head. Jesus does not say anything, so Simon pulls the anchor into the boat. "However, I will do as You say and let down the net."

I think James and John are curious to see what happens, and they follow us in their boat into the deeper water. When we throw the net onto the water, the lead weights begin to sink, and we pull on the cord, expecting an empty net. To our amazement, there is such an abundance of fish in the net that it begins to break. I look at Jesus, and He is standing there smiling. Did He really know all these fish were here, or was it just a lucky guess?

Simon calls to the boat next to us. His voice echoes over the water. "James! John! HELP! We have so many fish our nets are tearing! Hurry!"

With muscles straining and all of us working in unison, we fill both boats with musht, one of the most abundant and tastiest fish in the Sea of Galilee. I am glad we are as close to shore as we are because the weight of the fish causes the boat to tilt, allowing water to pour over the sides. Even though we are sinking, Simon is so overwhelmed that he falls at Jesus' knees and says he is not worthy to be in Jesus' presence.

I do not understand why Simon would make such a statement but am even more confused by Jesus' reply, "Do not be afraid, Simon. Starting now, you will be a fisher of men." What does He mean? Is Simon going to start catching men in his nets who fall overboard?

We finally get the boats to shore, and all the fishermen on shore start unloading the massive supply of fish. With that task completed, we go to cleaning the nets. The net used to catch all the fish is so damaged, it takes a long time to complete the tedious task of mending it.

We are so engrossed in what we are doing and tired we have not even missed Simon, Andrew, James, John, and Jesus. One of the worn-out and frustrated fishermen looks around. "Where did they go now? Does anyone know where they are?"

The remaining fishermen start searching for them when Joseph points at the horizon. "There they go." We watch our missing friends along with a multitude of people following Jesus as they walk out of sight.

I am tempted to run after them but am too tired. "What do we do now, Benjamin?"

"Let's finish folding these nets, and we will leave the fish with the remaining crew. I do not know about you boys, but I am exhausted.

Let's get some rest tonight and head home tomorrow unless we find our 'wandering friends' and have a change of plans. I am sure your fathers are wondering where we are and what we have been doing all this time."

# AN EVENTFUL RETURN HOME

After a night of tossing and turning, I wake up to sore and tired muscles, yet eager to see what today has in store for us. Unfortunately, we cannot find Jesus and the four missing fishermen anywhere, so Benjamin, Joseph, and I begin our journey home.

We sit quietly in the wagon, still exhausted from yesterday's activities. Breaking the silence, Benjamin asks, "What did you think about Jesus, boys? Do you think He is our Messiah?"

"I believe He could be," Joseph replies with extra emphasis on the word "could." "Although I have never seen a catch like we had yesterday after He told us where to cast our nets, I wish Jesus would have done something more convincing so I would know for sure. He is an incredible teacher, but I have not seen enough to forsake my family and our obligations to follow Him."

I shake my head. "What about all the things that Simon and Andrew told us. In addition to what we saw and heard, I believe He is our Messiah."

"I agree He is not your typical man-on-the-street, and their stories are incredible, but we did not really see anything out of the ordinary, Matthias. Jesus could have seen the school of fish and just pointed us in the direction they were heading. He was standing in the boat while we were seated."

"Did you notice when He was talking from the boat, no one had trouble hearing what He was saying? He was speaking in a normal tone, yet His voice projected, so everyone heard Him. There is something incredibly special about Him, Joseph." I am growing irritated with Joseph's disbelief. "I do not understand why you don't believe Him."

"I agree He is 'very special' and at least a prophet, but He has not convinced me He is the Messiah yet."

Benjamin has been sitting quietly while Joseph and I continue bickering back and forth. I guess we had been arguing longer than

I thought because we are approaching Capernaum. "You have been silent too long, Benjamin. What do you think?"

Before he can answer, we see a man with torn and dirty clothes, disheveled hair, and waving the veil used to cover a leper's mouth, hollering, "HE HEALED ME! I had leprosy, but now I AM CLEAN!"

Although people maintain the required "one-hundred feet safe distance from a leper rule," the wary crowd surrounding the man grows as he continues to recount what happened. We draw close enough to hear him excitedly say, "I asked Him if He could heal me, and Jesus of Nazareth touched me and said, 'Be healed.' Immediately the leprosy disappeared! Look at my skin—there is not a blemish or sore on it. I am clean!"

"The answer to your question is... Yes, I believe He is our Messiah," Benjamin declares as the healed man is lost in the crowd. "In fact, I think we may need to have a family meeting when we get home. I want to follow Jesus."

"Me, too, Benjamin." I look at Joseph to see if he has come to the same decision as Benjamin and I have. Not saying a word, He shrugs his shoulders.

After a few minutes of silence, Joseph replies, "I am torn about what to do. I want to follow Jesus if He is the Messiah, but I do not want to abandon our family responsibilities either. Our fathers cannot do everything."

"Boys, we need to be open and honest with Jesse, Seba, and the women. The main reason we made this trip was to find answers—I think we have. God provided food and water to our forefathers in the wilderness. He will provide for us to follow the Messiah, too. We just need a plan to present to the rest of the family."

We all fall silent for the remainder of our short journey to Bethsaida. I believe Jesus is the Messiah, and I want to learn everything I can about Him and from Him. My family has been so supportive of me since Arat and our baby died; I cannot leave them to run a business by themselves. Especially one as demanding as fishing. What am I going to do?

Arriving home several hours after sunset, Benjamin says, "Why don't you boys stay here tonight? We have all had time to think about things, and I would like to hear your thoughts so tomorrow we can present our plan to your parents." Benjamin adds with some hesitation, "I don't know exactly what I am going to say to her, but I am going to tell your aunt Elizabeth tonight so we can have her input, too."

Before we realize it, the sun is peeping over the horizon, and there is a knock on the door. "Who can that be at this hour?" Elizabeth asks as she opens the door to find Abba and Seba.

"We were about to go fishing and saw your wagon outside and the oil lamp burning. Since the boys did not come home last night, we wanted to make sure everything was alright." Abba grabs me, gives me a big hug, and asks with a smile, "How was the trip?"

"The trip went well, but we need to talk to you and your wives. We need to have a family meeting today." Abba and Seba scowl at Benjamin's reply.

"Don't worry. The boys continue to do an excellent job, but we need to make some changes and want to discuss them with all of the family present."

"What's happened?" Seba looks at each of our faces. "Talk to us!"

"We will tell you everything, but not until your wives are present to hear it. This is something which will affect them, too. Can we do it now?"

"The women are preparing to smoke some fish from yesterday's catch, but it should not prevent us from being able to talk." Abba looks at me with concern. "I wish I knew what this was about."

"It is going to be alright, Abba. We have a plan." I try to reassure him with a smile, but he does not seem to be too encouraged.

With Joseph and me following slowly, Abba and Seba lead the way into the courtyard where our mothers are starting the fire. Mother and Martha greet us with hugs and kisses but with worried looks on their faces as Seba announces we are about to have a family meeting. They enter the house while Joseph and I wait outside the door for Elizabeth and Benjamin since we have agreed Benjamin tells our parents the plan.

"We are all here. What is this meeting about?" Abba asks anxiously as Elizabeth and Benjamin step inside the house.

"Don't interrupt me until I finish with my spiel so I can keep all my thoughts together." Benjamin looks at each face of Joseph and my parents. "This is going to take a while."

Benjamin tells them how well Joseph and I have adapted to our new responsibilities and the progress we have made. Our parents smile proudly, and their worried looks vanish. They listen intently as Benjamin outlines our duties and the places we must visit to obtain the goods we need for the business and some new locations we are considering.

"The three of us agree the boys are ready to go alone now," Benjamin pauses and takes a deep breath before continuing, "which brings us to the main reason for this meeting—we need to ensure we have the family business covered at all times. One of us needs to be here to deliver fish to market and buy supplies. We can alternate between the three of us since we each want to follow Jesus. Each of us wants to either confirm or reaffirm his belief Jesus is the Messiah."

This draws gasps and "oh, no's" from our parents. Before they can express their opposition, Benjamin holds up his hand for them to be quiet and continues telling them what we have seen first-hand, from the baptism of Jesus to the huge catch of fish and the leper being healed. Then he gives a detailed report of what Simon and Andrew said they witnessed.

"Because we do not know how long we will have the opportunity to follow the Messiah, we have to act now while He is here. And as I told the boys, God provided for our forefathers in the wilderness, so He will provide for us now if Jesus is the Messiah. We do not expect you to accept this without some reservations, so let us hear your concerns." Benjamin concludes and sits down.

"I was afraid the boys would be easily persuaded by this man, but not you, Benjamin," Mother's voice quivers as she glares at Benjamin. "You were supposed to protect them from something like this happening."

"Rachel, I am as surprised as you are I want to follow this Man. He is no ordinary man. This Man has powers that can only be from God. People are being healed of all kinds of diseases at His command. Simon and Andrew have witnessed Him cast out demons with their own eyes. Power over evil must come from our Heavenly Father, and I believe that power will deliver our people from Roman oppression. I believe He is the Messiah."

"Mother, each of us made up our mind independently. Yes, I believe He is our Messiah, but Joseph is not as sure of it as Benjamin and I are. He wants to see and hear more before he decides. But if you could hear Jesus teach, see what He is doing, and how the people are reacting, I do not think you would be as resistant to the idea of us following Him. In fact, I think you would want to join us." Mother just shakes her head in disapproval but does not say anything.

Joseph clears his throat before speaking. "We have agreed Benjamin and Matthias go first to find and follow Jesus. I will stay home and help with the fishing, delivery, and exchange of fish for needed goods. Upon their return, we will swap so I can go see for myself what Jesus is doing and hopefully decide what I believe. None of us wants this to interfere with the family business and cause additional work for the other family members."

After several hours of discussion, Abba finally concedes, "I appreciate your consideration for being open and honest with us instead of abandoning us and the family business to follow Him. And

I know there is nothing I can say is going to change your minds. I see the determination and commitment on your faces. From what you have told us, you have seen and heard some amazing things. If only I could be certain this man is the Messiah, I would not have a problem with you following Him—in fact, I would join you." Mother groans and gives Abba a disapproving look.

Benjamin leans toward Mother and gently puts his hand on hers. "If we discover Him to be a fraud, we will immediately come home. But if we witness Him doing miracles and continuing to teach like we have already heard, we want you to join us and see for yourselves."

Joseph looks at his parents. "And remember, I still need some convincing before I commit to following Him. I believe He is at least a prophet, so hopefully, all of you will get to see Him soon, and you can provide insight. He is very convincing, though."

Once we are all in agreement, Elizabeth and Benjamin excuse themselves to go home to catch up on their lost sleep while Martha and Mother go outside to restart the fire. Since I was awake all night and we have lost the best "fishing hours" discussing the plans to follow Jesus, I am relieved to have my parents' support and am soon sound asleep.

# THE ENCOUNTER

Since our fathers lost an entire day of fishing because of us, Benjamin, Joseph, and I spend the next day fishing with them. By the end of the day and after a large catch, we mend the sails with the flax we purchased in Gennesaret. Within a couple of days, we have all the fish counted, smoked, stored, and ready for our next delivery.

Although we have heard many rumors where Jesus might be, Benjamin and I decide we will return to Capernaum in hopes that Jesus may have returned to His base. To support our mission in search of Jesus, we gather some of the smoked fish to trade for some needed supplies and begin our trek, much to my mother's dismay.

No sooner do we enter Capernaum than we hear a familiar voice bellow out, "Back again so soon, fellows?"

We reply in unison. "Hello, Simon."

"We have returned to find our Messiah." Benjamin hugs Simon. "Is He here? Do you know where He is?"

"As a matter of fact, He is here. The two of you must stay at my house while you are in town and join us, followers."

"Thank you, Simon. If you do not think it will be a problem, we graciously accept your offer." As we follow Simon to his home, we tell him of "the plan" presented to Joseph and my parents, along with their reactions and concerns.

"We are dining at the home of a new disciple of Jesus...a tax collector. He is expecting a large group, so two more people should not matter," Simon pauses to see our reaction.

Benjamin grimaces and strokes his beard. "A tax collector? As hated as tax collectors are among us Jews, and especially fishermen, Jesus is not going to make a favorable impression with them. You know the Jewish community considers most tax collectors traitors since they are Jews working for the oppressive Roman government. Plus, they get rich by making contracts with fishermen for the lease of fishing rights, overcharging them, and pocketing the excess money."

Simon nods in agreement. "I know, Benjamin. I felt the same way when I heard about it but give Him a chance. It is hard for us to understand, but Jesus is here to save all sinners. Including tax collectors."

Benjamin raises his eyebrows as if to say, "We will see," but does not say anything.

Toward evening, Simon, Benjamin, and I join Jesus and the remainder of His disciples on their way to the tax collector's home. "Shalom. Peace be with you." Jesus hugs Simon before greeting us. "Benjamin and Matthias, I am glad you are here to confirm your beliefs."

I want to ask how He knows why we are here, but my whole body is tingling when He hugs me. I am unable to move, much less speak. I gasp for air as the heavy burden of grief that has constantly been on my mind over the loss of Arat's and my son's lives is replaced with peaceful contentment. Jesus smiles as He looks at me—as if He knows what I am thinking and experiencing. He hugs Benjamin, then turns and begins walking to our destination, followed by the large group of mostly men.

"Come on, Matthias!" Benjamin calls back to me after seeing I am still motionless. "You don't want to be left behind."

I stumble as I try to walk. When the feeling returns to normal in my legs, I must run to catch Benjamin and the followers. "You don't seem to be having any trouble keeping up with the group, Benjamin. Are you alright?"

"I have never felt better, but I should be asking you the same thing. You look a little pale."

"When He hugged me, I had this strange sensation run through my body, and I could not move or speak for a while. I do not know how to explain it, but I immediately felt like a weight had been lifted, and I am whole again. Yes, I still miss them, but I no longer feel devastated about Arat and our son. He is our Messiah, Benjamin!"

"Yes, He is, Matthias." Benjamin continues to walk briskly without any effort. "I had the same feeling run through me, but now all my aches and pains are gone. I have not felt this well in years, if ever."

Jesus turns and looks at the two of us and smiles as if He has heard our entire conversation. But He couldn't have, could He? He is at the front of the group who is conversing noisily with each other, and we were not talking loudly. In fact, we were almost whispering.

The tax collector has prepared a huge pot of lamb stew and fresh bread. By the time we have finished eating, the news has spread about Jesus being there. So many people have entered the tax collector's home, there is no room for anyone else. Jesus takes advantage of this opportunity and begins preaching the word to them. Everyone listens in silence as He speaks.

Suddenly, there is a crackle on the roof as dried mud and straw begins falling into the room. The crowd pushes outward due to the falling debris with eyes fixed upon the ever-growing hole in the ceiling. The homeowner hollers at whoever is on his roof to stop and makes his way through the crowd. Before he can make it to the door, the hole is large enough to accommodate a man on a cot being lowered into the room. "Look what you have done to my roof. You will pay for this!"

Jesus touches the taxpayer's arm to calm him down. Simon leans toward Benjamin and me and whispers, "I recognize this man. He has been paralyzed since birth."

Jesus looks at the paralytic man as his cot reaches the floor. The man struggles to lean upon one elbow in order to more clearly see Jesus.

Jesus squats and reaches His hand toward him. "Son, your sins are forgiven."

Immediately behind me, there is murmuring from some of the scribes who interpret the Law. I overhear them saying Jesus is speaking blasphemies. Apparently, Jesus hears them, too, because He says, "Which is easier to say, 'Your sins are forgiven' or 'Rise, take up your bed and walk'?"

They do not respond.

"So that you know that the Son of Man has power on earth to forgive sins...." Jesus looks first at the scribes and then at the paralytic, then stands. "I say to you, rise, take up your bed, and go to your house."

All eyes are on the paralytic man, and there is a gasp from almost everyone present as he suddenly stands up straight and gathers his bed. I feel dizzy, and Simon grabs my arm to prevent me from falling.

With a broad smile, the elated man thanks Jesus, picks up his cot, exits the house through the middle of the crowd without even a limp, and rejoins his friends who are now standing outside. While some stand frozen in shock or rush from the house in fear, I stare in amazement for a moment. Then I fall on my knees at Jesus' feet, glorifying God along with many of His other followers. With a slight smile, Jesus stands in silence with His arms raised looking heavenly. His face is illuminated by the moonbeams entering the room through the damaged roof. I have never seen an angel that I know of, but this is how one must look.

Everyone reverently obeys when Jesus eventually tells everyone to go in peace. Simon, Benjamin, and I silently leave the house and are soon joined by Andrew, James, and John. Andrew breaks the silence. "It never ceases to amaze me what Jesus can do, even though we have seen some remarkable events." Simon, James, and John nod in agreement.

Before anyone else has a chance to talk, I excitedly disclose the overwhelming sensation I felt when Jesus' hugged me, how He seemed to know what I was thinking or feeling, and how He seemed to hear Benjamin and me proclaiming our belief over the noise of the group of followers. "Has anything similar happened to any of you?"

John nods. "He will not touch you very often, but when He does, you will feel differently. And although you see it happen frequently, you will never become accustomed to His ability to know your thoughts. It's as if He sees into your soul."

After saying good night to James, John, and Andrew, we enter Simon's house and are greeted by his wife, Febronia. Simon tells her about the events that just occurred. "After experiencing and seeing what you did today, what are your plans now, fellows? Any changes?"

"I wish Joseph could have been with us today because he would now be a believer, too." I look at Benjamin. "In fact, I wish our entire family was here. I am being selfish when I say I would like to spend all my time following Jesus, but that is not fair to you, Joseph, and to our family. They need to experience this, too."

"I feel the same way, Matthias. I thought we had everything figured out before we made this trip, but now I do not know what I... we are going to do. Especially if Joseph or any other family member feels the same way we do and wants to follow Jesus."

"Whatever you decide, you and your families are welcome anytime. Between Andrew's and my house, we can make room for your entire family whenever you are in this area for as long as you like."

Simon heads for bed as Benjamin and I reply in unison, "Thank you, Simon."

I cannot fall asleep because I continue thinking about all that has happened within the last few hours. I am torn between what I want to do and what I should do. I want to be a disciple of Jesus, but I should devote my time and energy to the family business. Or should I? Hopefully, Benjamin can advise me in the morning.

"Matthias, I have not slept any tonight, and I know you haven't either because I have heard you tossing and turning."

He does not wait for me to respond. "I have decided to return home in the morning to tell the family what we have witnessed, and it is up to you, but I would like for you to go back with me. The whole family needs to formulate a new plan, so Joseph and the remainder of the family have the opportunity to experience what you and I have experienced today."

"Although I would love to stay here, I think that is an excellent solution, Benjamin—the only solution. He is our Messiah, and we all need to be following Him."

"Now, try and get some sleep so we can leave as early as possible after daybreak,"

Feeling confident in our decision, I yawn and soon fall into a deep sleep.

# A REVISED PLAN

It seems like I just fell asleep when Benjamin is shaking me awake. "Get up, son. I hate to wake you since you were sleeping so peacefully, but we need to head home. It's getting late."

I look around and see it is already mid-morning, and the sun is shining through the open window. I yawn and stretch. "Thank you, Benjamin, for letting me sleep. Last night was the first night since Arat's death; I did not have any nightmares—in fact, I do not remember dreaming anything at all. I slept like a rock and actually feel rested."

"While you were asleep this morning, Simon woke me saying the multitude following Jesus is heading south. He did not know exactly where they were going or how long they would be there. I told him we were going home to talk to the family and will rejoin the group later."

"Hopefully, we can find them."

"The rumors circulating lately about Jesus' location have been fairly accurate, so we should be able to find them easily when we start searching again."

As the sunny skies quickly turn gray, we arrive in Bethsaida at the same time a storm is driving the fishermen to shore. Benjamin and I spot Joseph, Seba, and Abba already unloading the daily catch. Benjamin hops onboard the boat. "You boys need some help?" He lifts a large basket of fish without even a grunt.

"Be careful, Benjamin!" Abba orders. "That is too heavy for you!"

"It used to be, but I am a new man, Jesse. I am stronger and healthier than I have been in years. Or maybe, ever."

"Did you find some magic healing herbs?" Seba pokes at Benjamin.

"No! I found Jesus! Let me tell you about Him." Benjamin eagerly recounts his encounter with Jesus.

"You are moving a lot faster than you were, Benjamin," Seba cocks his head and raises his eyebrow. "But are you sure it was because Jesus healed you?"

"I immediately felt stronger and more energetic the moment He touched me. So yes, I believe. No, I know He healed me."

"And when He touched me, I had a tingling sensation all over my body. I could not even move or talk for a short time. I do not know how to explain it, but the emptiness I have been feeling since the death of Arat and our son was immediately filled with comfort. Plus, we saw Him heal a paralyzed man. That man stood, picked up his bed, and walked out of the house."

Teary-eyed, Abba grabs me and hugs me tightly. "Son, the joy on your face tells it all."

"If it were anyone else telling us these stories, I do not know if I would believe them." Abba looks at Benjamin from head to toe. "And seeing you moving better than I have ever seen you move, I have no doubt that the two of you are telling us the truth."

Seba winks at Benjamin. "Let's go see what Elizabeth thinks of her 'new' husband. She is probably still helping Rachel and Martha smoke fish, so let us head home and surprise the women before the storm comes ashore. We are finished here anyway, thanks to Benjamin's newfound strength."

We all laugh, but Benjamin is already spryly walking toward home and looks back. "While we are all together, we need to have another family meeting. We have a lot to discuss."

As we arrive at the house, the skies empty, and Benjamin runs inside. Elizabeth looks at him in shock as he grabs her and swings her around. "What happened to you?"

I sit silently and in awe as Benjamin eloquently relates every detail of his healing and our encounter with Jesus. "I would like for all of us to have the opportunity to meet our Messiah as soon as possible. Simon and Andrew can accommodate all of us at their homes in Capernaum, so we already have a place to stay. Through mutual contacts, they will send word to me when they return to their homes."

I cannot conceal my enthusiasm. "Please, everyone! Take advantage of this opportunity to get to meet Jesus! Watch Him and listen to Him because you will not regret it!"

Abba laughs at me as I feel my face redden. "Maybe we should go. I would like to see Him in person and form my own opinion. We already have a large supply of smoked fish on hand and will have even more as soon as we prepare today's catch. Hopefully, we can catch some additional ones before we hear from Simon."

Even Mother approves of the idea. "We always respect your opinion, Benjamin, but tonight you certainly are convincing. And I have never seen Matthias this committed and excited about anything. And the smile on his face is a welcome sight." She hugs me. "It would be nice to get away for a few days, too."

When everyone leaves, Mother tells me to sit down. "Matthias, Benjamin did all the talking tonight, and you did not get to say much. You are so excited about this Jesus I want to hear in your words exactly what happened in Capernaum. Do not leave anything out. In fact, tell me about every encounter you have had with this Man from the first time you saw Him. I want to know as many facts about Him as I can, and I know I can depend on you for that."

Abba sits down with us as I begin. "This is going to take a while." And it does. We sit by candlelight and talk well into the night as I recall every minute detail of my association with Jesus. I am surprised I remember so much.

"He does perform miraculous fetes and has extraordinary powers. Hopefully, we will get to see Him perform some of these miracles." Mother kisses me on the cheek and heads for bed. "Thank you for sharing your experiences with us."

"The miracles are extraordinary, but don't let that be the only thing you see. Watch Him and how He presents Himself. Listen to what He says and watch the crowd's reaction. The way He looks and speaks is as impressive as the miracles."

"I have to say, son, I am excited about meeting Him" Abba puts his arm around my shoulder. "I have been hearing so many rumors I did not know what to believe...until now. I believe He is our Messiah, and I think your mother does, too. She just has not said it yet."

All my life, my parents have influenced me, and I am elated God is working through me to influence them. "I am glad you told me that, Abba." I give him a hug. "Knowing we as a family are united makes following Jesus less stressful for me. I know many families are divided. I have overheard several followers talking about their families disowning them because they are following Jesus. I do not know what I would do if I did not have your and Mother's support."

After several days of fishing, we have a larger supply of smoked fish to trade than normal. We have even mended all our sails and nets. Benjamin gets word Simon has returned home and has suggested we come as soon as possible. We spend the remainder of the afternoon loading smoked fish onto Benjamin's wagon and gathering food and other items for our journey.

Simon and his wife, Febronia, welcome us warmly into their home. After exchanging introductions and greetings, Simon looks at Benjamin and me. "Jesus has performed more unbelievable miracles these past couple of weeks. Please sit."

"I am assuming you fellows have told your family of the miracles He had performed as of when you were last here." Benjamin and I both nod.

I cannot wait to hear about them and lean in closer. "What has He done now?"

Simon clears his throat. "We went to the region of the Gerasenes, and when Jesus got out of the boat, a man with an unclean spirit who lived in the tombs of the cliffs howled like a wolf and ran up to

Him. Jesus did not flinch. This man was the wildest looking person or animal I have ever seen."

Simon looks at me. "You thought John the Baptist looked wild. This man made him look like a king. He was drooling like a mad dog. Townspeople had tried to chain him, but he was too strong for them. The iron shackles were still around his wrists and ankles, but the chains were broken—they were not strong enough to subdue him. He had torn them apart, and they clanged together as he jumped around. Dried blood covered his naked, dirty body, where he had cut himself with sharp stones. His eyes twitched from side to side as he looked at Jesus. He bowed directly in front of Jesus like an abused dog and screamed loudly in a hoarse, guttural voice. "What have I to do with you, Jesus the Son of the Most High God? Do not torment me!"

We all sit wide-eyed, listening to Simon.

"Jesus calmly replied for the unclean spirit to come out of the man and asked him his name. He said his name was Legion because he had many demons. The devils begged Jesus to send them into a nearby herd of swine feeding on the mountain. When Jesus did, the demons entered the pigs, and they all rushed down to the sea and drowned—there must have been more than a thousand pigs."

Benjamin chuckles. "I bet the herdsmen were not happy about that."

"Not happy is an understatement. They immediately ran and reported it to the townspeople. When the herdsmen returned with the people, and they saw the wild man sitting, clothed and in his right mind and the mountain of dead pigs in the water, they begged Jesus to leave the area. The man wanted to follow Jesus, but Jesus told him to go to his family and tell them the 'great things the Lord had done.' He did as Jesus commanded, telling everyone he saw as we watched him run out of sight."

We all sit in stunned silence while Simon takes a sip of water. "If you thought that miracle was amazing, wait until you hear about this one."

"We boarded the boat and crossed over to the other side of the sea, and a large crowd gathered around Jesus when He went ashore. Jairus, one of the synagogue officials, fell at Jesus' feet crying. He pleaded desperately for Jesus to lay His hands on his daughter, who was sick to the point of death, so she would get well. As Jesus and the crowd followed Jairus to his house, Jesus suddenly stopped and turned. He asked who touched the hem of His garment. Sometimes I am too quick to speak."

We laugh when Febronia interrupts. "Most of the time."

Simon blushes. "I comment that with the crowd pressing in around us, why did He ask who touched Him. It could have been anyone. He ignored my question and asked again who touched His garment."

"A frail, thin woman slowly came and fell down before Jesus trembling. She admitted to touching Him and said she had been hemorrhaging for twelve years—physicians could not cure her. When she heard about Jesus' healing powers, she thought if she could just touch His clothing, she would be well. She said when she touched Him, the blood flow stopped, and she was healed of her suffering. Jesus said her faith had made her whole and to go in peace—she was rid of her plague."

"While He was speaking, the ruler of the synagogue's house approached Jairus and told him his daughter had died and there was no need to trouble the Master. Jesus told Jairus to not be afraid and believe. Only James, John, and I were the only ones allowed into the house. A large group of mourners was already inside, and they laughed at Jesus when He asked why they were crying—the damsel was only sleeping. He made everyone leave except Jairus and his wife and the three of us. We entered the room where she was lying."

"The girl looked to be maybe eleven or twelve years old and was obviously dead. They had not even closed her eyes, and they were blankly staring into space. She had already turned grayish-blue."

I do not need to turn my head to know Abba and Mother are watching me to see my reaction to the description of the dead child. Although it brings back bad memories, I do not feel the emptiness I would have prior to Jesus touching me.

"Jesus took the girl by the hand and said, 'Damsel, arise.' The girl immediately stood, was hugged by her parents, and exited the room. You should have seen the looks on the face of the people who only moments before had laughed at Jesus."

I speak without thinking. "I wish Jesus had been around when Arat and my son died."

Simon kneels beside me. "I'm sorry, Matthias. I should not have been so descriptive. I was not thinking—again."

I smile at him. "It would have been a problem for me before I met Jesus, but now it's not."

# GETTING TO KNOW HIM

Benjamin leans over and touches Simon's arm. "Why the urgency in our arrival, Simon?"

"The other day, we were met by hundreds of people who followed us up onto a mountain. Jesus' notoriety has become so widespread there were people from Galilee, Decapolis, Jerusalem, Judaea, and beyond the Jordan River. Many of them brought their sick family members and friends for Jesus to heal. Not only did He heal them, but He taught the massive crowd key lessons on daily living and what traits are pleasing to God—humility, meekness, and kindness. He contradicted some of the lessons we have been taught by the priests and traditions we have practiced for generations. He told us to be forgiving instead of practicing the long custom of 'an eye for an eye and a tooth for a tooth.' And we should love our enemies instead of hating them."

"Although we are all familiar with prayer, Jesus taught us prayer should not be vain repetitions. They should not be public for others to see and hear but be private and personal for only God to see and hear." Simon talks non-stop for several minutes, giving more details of Jesus' teaching.

Simon takes a deep breath before finally answering Benjamin's question. "Because Jesus is becoming more famous each day and unable to get out in public without being bombarded by them, I wanted all of you to meet Him face-to-face and get to know Him personally as soon as possible."

Just as Simon gets the words "as soon as possible" out of his mouth, there is a knock on the open door. Standing in the doorway is the silhouette of a man. Although we cannot distinguish any features, I know it is Jesus. "Shalom. Peace be with all of you." Jesus walks to where Benjamin and I are standing and greets us with a hug. "Welcome back!"

Like before, I am frozen in place and cannot move or speak as Jesus walks over to my parents and hugs them. "Welcome, Jesse and Rachel. I am glad Matthias brought his parents this trip." Stunned that Jesus knows their names, they are unable to speak. He proceeds to Elizabeth, Joseph, and his parents, greets each with a warm embrace, and calls each of them by name.

After He greets Simon and Febronia, we are all finally able to move again when Jesus motions for us to sit down. "I know some of you have never seen or heard me before and have questions about my true identity, but you have heard about Me. Hopefully, by the time you return home, you will know Me. God did not send his Son into the world to condemn it but to save the world through Him. Light has now come into this world. Those who do evil love darkness and hate the light, but those who do truth come to the light. Seek the Light!"

We all sit motionless as He stands. "Now, I must go about my Father's business."

Jesus smiles, waves goodbye, and walks out the open door.

For a moment, we all sit quietly, staring at the open door. I finally break the silence. "By now, you probably know that was Jesus. Since you have seen and been touched by Him, what do you think now?"

Seba shakes his head. "I am not convinced He is our Messiah. For me to believe, I am going to have to witness Him do something special."

Simon is quick to respond, "He already has. Without telling Jesus you were coming, He came here and called each of you by name. In fact, He told you the reason you were here."

He gets no response from Seba.

"He not only knew our names, but He knew we are Matthias' parents. He also knew some of us have doubts about Him." Abba looks at Seba and Joseph, but they still do not respond.

Mother places her hand on my shoulder and looks into my eyes. "Standing in the doorway, I knew who He was even though I had never seen Him before. And when He touched me and looked into my eyes, I felt like He knew everything about me. It was scary how exposed I felt, but I have no doubt He is who He claims to be."

"I feel the same way, Rachel," Martha turns toward Seba and Joseph. "I don't understand your doubt, but that is a decision you have to make. What do you think, Elizabeth?"

"After what Benjamin had told me, I was a believer before I met Him. Meeting Him only confirms His identity to me. His whole demeanor is holy. His message was brief but complete. He did not have to say another word for me to know who He is and what He meant."

Everyone continues to converse about meeting Jesus—everyone except Joseph and Seba, who both remain silent. Seeing Joseph slip out the door, I follow him outside. "You have not said a word. Are you alright?"

When he shrugs as if to say he does not know, I ask, "What do you think? Talk to me, Joseph."

He opens his mouth like he wants to speak, but nothing comes out. He shakes his head and mouths, "I cannot talk right now."

He glances around as if looking for answers, still saying nothing, and quickly turns, walks a short distance away, and sits under a fig tree. I watch him for a little while, but he never looks up. His knees are pulled up to his chest, and he is resting his forehead on his arms. Not knowing what to do, I go back inside the house so he can have some time alone.

After a few minutes, Seba asks me where Joseph is, and I tell him he is down the street sitting under a tree. "He was acting strangely and would not talk to me. I watched him for a little while to make sure he was all right, but he seemed to be distant and lost in thought. I suppose he just needs some time to think about all that has happened."

Seba's response is loud enough for everyone to hear and draws glances from everyone as he walks out the door. "It is a lot to absorb. Frankly, I could use some time alone, too. I will go see how he is doing."

Seba and Joseph reenter the house a while later, and both are smiling. Joseph scans the faces of everyone before speaking. "When Jesus hugged me and looked into my eyes, I could not speak. I thought it was just a momentary thing like Matthias said happened to him. But while all of you were talking, I realized I really had lost my voice. I was not scared but was very confused and did not know what else to do, so I went outside to think. Although I wanted to talk to Matthias and to Father when he first came outside, I could not make a sound. Not until I told Father I am now a believer."

Seba puts his arm around Joseph's shoulder. "And I believe, too. I guess that is the sign I needed to assure me that Jesus is our Messiah."

"I knew all of you would eventually see the Light." Simon gives Seba and Joseph a warm embrace. "I did not realize it would be this soon, though. Welcome, brothers and sisters in Christ." We all share a hug and excitedly recount the events of the day.

The next few days, we follow Jesus tirelessly throughout the area. We watch and listen to Him, trying to absorb everything that He says and does.

Because of the oppression of the Jews by the Romans, we find it odd a Roman centurion would come alone into a group of Jews without the protection of at least some of the one hundred soldiers under his command. Apparently, he is of high rank—medals of bravery are glistening on his harness, and the crest on his silver helmet is very ornate. A blue cloak is thrown around his shoulders, and he is carrying the vine-like stick as a measure of his rank. The centurion tells Jesus he is not worthy to have Jesus in his home but to speak the word, and his servant with palsy will be healed. I assume his servant must be a Jew and has told the centurion of Jesus' powers; otherwise, how would a Roman soldier know. Jesus is so impressed He states He has not found anyone with so great a faith in Israel and for him to go his way. He adds, "As you have believed, so it is done unto you."

I have seen Jesus heal someone in front of Him, but can He really heal someone that He cannot see? Are His powers that strong?

Another day, two blind men cry out to Jesus to have mercy on them. Jesus asks them if they believe He can restore their sight, and both men reply, "Yea, Lord." Jesus touches their eyes. "According to your faith, be it unto you." When their sight is restored, I must laugh at the expressions of shock by my parents and especially Seba—his mouth flies open as he staggers backward. I think he would have fallen if Joseph had not caught him. This is the first miracle they have witnessed. Jesus tells the two men to tell no one, but of course, they cannot keep from telling everyone they meet, and Jesus' fame is spread throughout the area.

So much so a dumb man possessed by a devil is brought to Jesus. When Jesus casts out the devil, some Pharisees say He is casting out devils through the prince of devils. The Pharisees have been teaching us about the coming Messiah. Why don't they recognize Him?

Jesus quickly tells them a kingdom divided against itself cannot stand, so why would Satan revolt against himself and be divided. The Pharisees are dumbfounded and have no response, except for public embarrassment.

As we enter the gate of the city of Nain, we witness a large group of mourners carrying the dead body of a young man for burial. We are told the diseased who died early this morning was the only son of the distraught woman closely following the corpse. And her husband died recently as well, so she is now alone. Jesus approaches the woman and tells her in a soothing voice to not weep. What is He doing? She has just lost and is about to bury her only son on top of just losing her husband—of course, she is going to cry. I understand and share her feelings. It makes me feel like crying, too.

Jesus turns toward the dead body. "Young man, arise."

I should not be surprised at anything Jesus can do, but everyone is stunned when the dead man sits up and begins to talk. Although

I am scared too, I am amused at how frightened some of the people are. We are almost trampled by some of them running away in fear. Nothing seems impossible for Him. He even has power over death.

When Jesus calls twelve of His disciples and ordains them as apostles, four of them are Simon, Andrew, James, and John. I am happy for the four of them but do not understand why Jesus selected some of the other apostles. Surprisingly, Matthew, the former tax collector, is ordained. Although he walked away from collecting taxes, he is still disliked by many of the Jews in the area who know and recognize him. There is also a zealot named Simon, a Galilean who wants to overthrow the Roman government by force. Is Jesus wanting to build an army to overthrow the Roman government? The remainder of "The Twelve" are all from Galilee except one Judean, Judas Iscariot.

"It's an honor just to be chosen by Jesus to be an apostle. He has given us power to heal diseases and to cast out demons. He is sending the twelve of us to 'preach that the kingdom of heaven is at hand,' 'to repent,' and 'to heal the sick,' so I'm going to be away for a few days," Simon explains.

We congratulate Simon on his new position, and I ask if we can go with him. Simon responds with truly little confidence in his new role. "You can if you like. But since we are going to be the ones teaching instead of Jesus, you may want to wait until you can be with Him. Jesus told us not to worry about what we would say because the Spirit of our Father will speak in us. I hope that is true. As loud and spontaneous as I am, I am not a great speaker like He is."

# A HUNGRY CROWD

United in our belief Jesus is the Messiah, my family thanks Simon and Febronia for their hospitality and takes Simon's advice to return home and assume our everyday activities. We wait impatiently for Simon to notify us of the apostles' arrival so we can rejoin Jesus and His disciples.

A couple of weeks pass before we receive word from Simon that Jesus and "The Twelve" are coming to the Bethsaida area to get some much-needed rest. Jesus wants some solitude and time to grieve after hearing John the Baptist was beheaded by Herod Antipas as a gift to his daughter. We are instructed to not tell anyone of His arrival.

Benjamin and Elizabeth, Joseph and his parents, my parents and I decide to meet them. But we are not the only ones. It apparently was not a well-kept secret because when Jesus and "The Twelve" arrive by boat, there is a very larger group of people already waiting on the shore.

Jesus looks tired but leads all of us who have gathered on the shore, along with many more who join us along the way, to an open area where we are told to sit on the ground. I wave to Simon, and he motions for us to join him, Andrew, and their parents, and the other apostles who are sitting at Jesus' feet. When we greet the two apostles and their parents, Jesus gives us a warm, welcoming smile as we sit on the ground.

Like the time Jesus taught from the fishing boat to the crowd gathered onshore at Gennesaret, He speaks in a normal tone, and even those farthest away among the throng gathered seem to have no problem hearing Him. Everyone, including the children, sits quietly and listens intently as He tells us about the kingdom of God.

We sit mesmerized as Jesus heals one person after another with various diseases and ailments. Those who are unable to come to Him on their own are assisted by friends or family, while many are brought to Him on cots. Some have deformities that immediately disappear at His command.

Hours pass quickly, and the approach of evening seems to go unnoticed by the crowd. No one is leaving. However, "The Twelve" are concerned, and I overhear the apostles as they confront Jesus. "You need to send the multitude away so they can go into the nearby towns and find food and lodging. It is getting late."

Jesus is not alarmed. "There is no need to send them away. Feed them."

"With what? We have no food." Philip, who is one of "The Twelve," sounds agitated. "We are in a deserted place, and there is nowhere for us to buy bread even if we had the money, especially for all these people."

Jesus looks at him calmly. "Go through the crowd and see if anyone has any food."

While Jesus continues healing the sick, the apostles wander through the multitude in search of food. They look defeated when they return. Andrew and a young boy carrying a basket approach Jesus. "All we found is this one lad with five barley loaves and two small fish. What is that among so many people?"

Jesus smiles broadly and squats beside the lad, puts His arm around him, and thanks him for sharing his food. Jesus instructs the apostles to have everyone sit in groups of fifty, and as we move to join others to form a group, Abba leans over and whispers. "What do you think Jesus is going to do now?"

"A miracle."

All eyes are upon Jesus as He takes the loaves, lifts them skyward, and prays. "Thank you, Father, for supplying our daily bread."

The young boy, along with everyone else, curiously watches as Jesus begins breaking the bread. He takes one of the fish, raises it toward heaven, blesses it, and breaks it in half. My parents are wide-eyed as the bread and fish multiply while Jesus continues looking upward and tearing the bread and fish into bite-size pieces and giving it to the apostles to distribute among the mass of people.

Although everyone on the hill has witnessed the miracles of healing today, reactions vary to the amount of food being produced from the five loaves and two fish. Some are skeptical of eating it until they have seen others do so without consequence. Others gorge themselves as if it is their last meal. Most of the crowd eats quietly and watches in awe as Jesus continues to produce more bread and fish.

As Simon delivers our portion of the bread and fish, he leans over between Benjamin and me. "We have over a hundred groups of fifty sitting on this hill to be fed. That is over five thousand people."

Jesus repeats the process with the bread and fish until everyone eats and no longer wants more. He commands the apostles to gather up the fragments that remain so that nothing is wasted. I do not know where the baskets come from, but "the Twelve" each fill one with the leftovers.

After the crowd experiences this miracle by Jesus, some start saying Jesus is the one Moses prophesied about. "We need to make him our king!"

I watch the multitude as this thought spreads throughout the crowd, and they become more boisterous and forceful. The disciples move between the crazed mass and Jesus as if they could protect Him from the mob. When I look to see what Jesus' response will be, to my amazement, He is nowhere to be seen. He was there just a moment ago. Where did He go?

When "The Twelve" finally convince the frenzied throng Jesus is no longer here, some are angry and demand to know His whereabouts, while others search earnestly for Him calling His name and looking behind rocks, bushes, and trees on the hillside. Some wander about not knowing where to go—like sheep without a shepherd, and others gather their belongings and begin their journeys home.

Simon whispers to my family as he passes. "Jesus instructed us to get in the boat and meet Him on the other side toward Capernaum. Do you mind if my parents and James' and John's parents join you on your return home? Since it will be after dark when they get there, I would prefer they did not travel alone."

"We would be happy for them to join us." Seba puts one arm around Jona's shoulder and the other around the shoulder of Zebedee, the father of James and John. "We will make sure they get home safely."

I have not interacted with Zebedee since the day James and John abandoned their jobs and left unannounced to follow Jesus. That encounter with Zebedee was not too pleasant for me, and I am not too happy he will be joining us on our homeward journey. However, I am pleasantly surprised when he offers a warm apology. "Please forgive me for my abrupt behavior the other week. It was not like my boys to abandon their jobs and walk away like they did. Now that I understand why, I am deeply sorry for the way I acted. Forgive me."

We embrace and talk almost constantly the entire way home about the miracles we have witnessed and heard about. As Simon said, it is well after dark when we arrive. After Zebedee, Jona, and their wives are left at their doorsteps; Benjamin approaches Joseph and me. "Since I have the renewed strength and endurance of my youth, why don't the two of you follow Jesus full-time while I resume my former duties in the family business."

I stare at him in shock. "Don't you want to follow Jesus, too?"

"We all do, Matthias. But while you were engrossed in conversation with your new best friend, Zebedee...." Benjamin pauses and laughs at his own joke. "Your parents and I discussed it and felt with you boys' vigor and enthusiasm, the two of you are the most capable to maintain the necessary pace to be effective disciples. I am feeling spry now, so I will join you on some of my trade excursions."

Abba chimes in. "Hopefully, we can incorporate some of our fishing trips around Jesus' ministry, too...and have some family time together."

Although disappointed Joseph and I are the only ones of our family who will be traveling with Jesus and His followers, I am grateful and touched by my family's willingness to make the sacrifices allowing us to do so. Joseph and I quickly make plans for our departure so we can spend as much quality time as possible with our parents, not knowing when we will see them again.

# KEEPING YOUR HEAD ABOVE WATER

Shortly after sunrise, Joseph lightly knocks on the door. My parents tearfully bid us goodbye, and we begin our journey to Capernaum. It is reassuring to know I have my family's blessing.

When we arrive at Simon's house, Febronia tells us Peter and Andrew are at the temple with Jesus. We climb the steps, enter the massive doors to the stone structure, and find a large crowd surrounding Jesus. "I am the bread of life. He who comes to Me shall never hunger, and he who believes in Me shall never thirst. If anyone eats of this bread, he will live forever; the bread I give is My flesh, which I shall give for the life of the world."

I am confused and glimpse at Joseph. He has the same bewildered look I must have and shrugs his shoulders. Many of the Jews around us start grumbling they know He is the son of Joseph and Mary, and they do not practice cannibalism. Does He really expect us to eat His flesh?

Jesus reiterates, "Whoever eats My flesh and drinks My blood has eternal life, and I will raise him up at the last day."

I am not eating the flesh or drinking the blood of anyone. Apparently, many of His followers feel the same way because the number of Jesus' disciples dramatically decreases as many of them exit the temple shaking their heads—in either confusion, disbelief, or both.

"How could we have been so foolish as to believe this man was our Messiah?"

"Eat his flesh...drink his blood. Who does he think we are?"

Although Joseph and I believe Jesus is our Messiah, we look at each other perplexed. Surely, He does not literally mean what He is saying. But what does He mean? Maybe Simon and Andrew can explain it to us later. For now, I have no idea what He is talking about.

Jesus does not seem concerned He lost so many disciples. He asks "the Twelve" if any of them wants to also leave, and they all shake their heads no. Simon answers, "Who shall we go to? You have the words of eternal life. You are the Christ, the Son of the living God."

After Jesus finishes teaching the few people who remained and the crowd disperses, we join Simon and Andrew as they leave the temple. "Joseph and I don't understand what Jesus meant when He said to eat His flesh and drink His blood. Can you explain it to us?"

Simon stops and stands still to explain. "Flesh and blood are essential for the human body to exist. It requires food and drink to grow and mature. The same is true for the spiritual body. The spiritual body must be fed for it to mature and grow. Jesus' teaching and example are the sources of that nourishment. He was not promoting cannibalism like many of the people who left were thinking. He was simply stating we must feed on Him—His teaching to have eternal life."

"I guess that makes sense. But why didn't Jesus simply say that? All those people would have understood what He meant and would still be following Him."

Andrew steps between us and puts his arms around our shoulders as we begin walking down the temple steps. "As you are around Jesus more, you will realize He sometimes uses everyday things and events to describe heavenly lessons. Sometimes the message is clear. Other times it is like solving a riddle. He wants us to meditate and ponder on His teaching and to solve that riddle on our own. But once we know the answer, the true meaning of His message is obvious and applicable. We are not just hearing what He is saying but thinking about and understanding what He means."

Simon clears his throat. "Since we are explaining Jesus' teaching to you, Andrew and I have already talked about this...and if you are going to be His disciples, we want to mentor both of you and share with you what Jesus teaches to the apostles."

"Would you do that, Simon? I would love for you to teach me as much about Jesus as you can."

"Me too!" Joseph echoes.

"Although we will work as a group when feasible, there will be times when that will not be possible. We will have to tell one of you something." Simon looks from my face to Joseph's. "Then the two of you can share information with each other."

Joseph and I nod in agreement. "We can do that."

Simon's expression changes from one of enthusiasm and welcome to be part of this movement to a somber and grim look. "Jesus has warned 'The Twelve' of the consequences of following Him, so you need to know this before you commit yourself totally to be a disciple of His. You have already seen the opposition to Jesus by the Pharisees, and eventually, they will be cornered and fight back. Be prepared for threats from those in power."

"Jesus has also warned us of public ridicule and physical harm, including death. We are all lucky to have our family's support. Many followers are already being scorned and alienated by the ones they love—their families. The ultimate reward is Heaven, so we must endure whatever we are faced with on earth. Are you ready and willing to accept the challenge? You do not have to answer that question right now but be prepared too soon."

Scared of the possible consequences but convicted by my beliefs, I want to accept the challenge. But am I willing to fight or suffer for them? I do not know.

We walk silently the remainder of the way to Simon's house. As we approach the door, Andrew breaks the silence. "Get Simon to tell you what happened to him last night. You will not believe it."

"Come in with us, Andrew. You might have something you want to add...or have a different perspective on what happened than I do. This is going to take a while, so make yourselves comfortable."

Simon greets Febronia as Joseph and I anxiously sit at his feet. "We were in the middle of the sea at the fourth watch of night when a huge storm caught us by surprise. The wind was gusting, and we were struggling to keep the boat upright. The boat was being tossed to and fro by the waves and taking on water, and some of us had tied ourselves to the boat to keep from being washed overboard. It was even worse than your first night-fishing trip."

Simon winks at me, and we all laugh. "We were all startled— actually, we were all scared—when we saw something strange approaching us on top of the water. It is funny now that I think back on it because some of us cried out in fear like little girls." When Simon and Andrew stop laughing, he continues. "It had the form of a man, but facial features were unrecognizable because of the blowing rain and mist from the waves. Its white robe was blowing in the wind like a flag as it calmly approached us. We thought it was a spirit walking on the waves."

Joseph and I both gasp. "What was it?"

"We heard a voice say, 'Be of good cheer! It is I; do not be afraid.' I recognized the voice—it was Jesus."

Confused, I shake my head to try to think more clearly. "It was Jesus? He was walking on the water? How did He do that?"

Andrew interrupts. "Wait until you hear the rest of this story. It gets even more amazing."

"I asked Him, 'Lord, if it is You, command me to come to You on the water,' and He said, 'Come.' I obeyed Him and crawled over the side of the boat."

"You did *what?*"

"When my feet touched the water, it felt solid like I was on the ground. But after a couple of steps toward Jesus, I realized I was also walking on the stormy sea and became terrified. When I lost focus and took my eyes off Him, I began to sink and cried out for Him to save me. Jesus reached out and caught me by the hand before I completely sank and said, 'Oh you of little faith, why did you doubt?' He walked me to the boat, and when we climbed into it, the wind immediately stopped blowing, the sea became calm, and the clouds disappeared to reveal a clear starry night."

"You actually walked on the water? What was that like?" Joseph is as curious as I am.

"It was no different than walking on land as long as I kept my attention on Jesus. However, I thought I was going to drown when I started sinking, but He caught me before I even sank knee-deep."

"When they got into the boat, we all professed that Jesus is the Son of God. As many miracles I have seen, this was one of the most incredible things to watch." Andrew punches Simon in the shoulder with a mischievous smile." I guess because my big brother was doing something that is not humanly possible. Seriously though, not only does Jesus have dominion over the wind and seas, but at His command, He gave Simon special powers to walk on water."

"I'm flabbergasted! Jesus walked on water!" I lay back, trying to absorb what I have just heard. "And you did, too! I wish I could have been there to see that."

"I will see all of you tomorrow, but I need to be getting home to see my wife. You can stay at our house if you want to, Joseph. It will give us time to talk some more." Andrew stands and pats me on the shoulder. "The color is gone from your face, Matthias. How are you feeling?"

I look up at Andrew. His eyebrows are drawn together as he leans in to get a closer look at me. "I'm fine...or think I am. I know what the two of you told me is true, but it is so unbelievable. I am just having trouble comprehending it. What is He going to do next?"

# A TOUR OF THE REGION

Over the next several months, Simon and Andrew mentor us as we travel with "the Twelve" and numerous other disciples. It is miraculous how God provides for His children when we do His will. All our family's needs have been met or exceeded. Daniel, one of Elizabeth's nephews, along with his wife Esther and newborn son, moved to Bethsaida from Jericho to join our family's fishing business, relieving some of the duties in Joseph's and my absence. Benjamin continues to have renewed strength and is performing more physical labor, as well as making all the business trips.

I realize the benefits of the roles of fishermen in Jesus' ministry as we sail to the Greek-speaking region of Tyre and Sidon. Not only do fishermen provide a means of transportation to distant areas along the coast of the Sea of Galilee and have reliable contacts in most of the desired destinations, but they also can speak some of the native dialects in each of these areas.

Jesus wants no one to know of His presence while there, but the knowledge of His arrival precedes Him. A Canaanite woman pulling her resistant daughter keeps following Him, asking Jesus to cast out a demon that possesses her. The daughter, who is maybe six years old, looks disheveled. Her hair is knotted, her tunic is torn, and she has piercing, evil-looking eyes which dart from one person to another. Jesus responds by saying He is sent to save the Jews, "the lost sheep of Israel," and not the Gentiles and even refers to the Gentiles as "little dogs." The woman does not seem offended and continues to be respectful. And persistent. She cleverly responds even the "little dogs" eat the crumbs which fall from their masters' tables. The girl struggles to pull away from her mother, but the mother has a firm grip. Seeing her faith in Him, Jesus removes the demon from her daughter with a single command. The girl instantly calms and stands staring at Jesus as the mother gratefully kneels before Him.

His presence is publicized even more, so we depart from the region. The multitudes are unavoidable as we enter the region of Decapolis on the eastern shore of the Sea of Galilee. Although it is hard to understand what he is saying, a deaf man with a speech impediment is brought to Jesus and begs Him to be healed. Jesus puts his fingers in the man's ears, spits, and touches his tongue and looks up to heaven, and says, "Be opened!" The man immediately jerks his head toward whoever calls him by name. He smiles and responds clearly. "I heard that... I can hear!" His impediment is gone. I never understand why Jesus commands those being healed to tell no one, but like that man, I would proclaim it for all to hear, too.

Even though most of the inhabitants of this area are Gentile and worship the Greek gods, several thousand surround Jesus to hear Him teach. At the end of the third day, Jesus gathers The Twelve around Him away from the crowd. "I do not want to send these people away hungry. How many loaves do you have?"

They produce seven loaves and a few fish, which they give to Him knowing what is about to occur. Much like the feeding of the five thousand where my parents were present, Jesus gives thanks for the loaves and fish, breaks them, and gives to the apostles to distribute throughout the crowd. When all are full, seven large baskets full of the fragments remain, and Jesus sends away the multitude. Unlike the five thousand, this crowd leaves peacefully.

We sail to Magdala, and I watch in surprise as Simon slips a small sword underneath his cloak. I tilt my head and raise my eyebrows but do not need to ask the obvious question. What is he doing with a sword? He notices I am watching and points to the shore. "This may be what Jesus warned us about. It does not hurt to be prepared." He quickly hurries to Jesus' side.

As Jesus disembarks, He is immediately confronted by the ruling class of Israel—the Sadducees and the Pharisees. The Sadducees are governed by the written Torah and are the wealthy and most powerful group consisting of the chief priest, the high priest, and the majority of the seventy seats of the ruling council called the Sanhedrin. They are more interested in maintaining good relations with the Roman government rather than with the Jewish people. The Pharisees, on the other hand, accept the entire written Word as inspired by God along with the oral Torah that is man-made. They hold the minority of seats even though they are more relatable to the common Jew. The two groups also have differing opinions on the resurrection of the dead, the afterlife, and belief in angels and demons.

For the Pharisees and Sadducees to be united and here together is very uncharacteristic because of their long-standing rivalry over social and religious issues. But together, they are challenging Jesus to do miracles and demanding a "sign from heaven." However, Jesus is not intimidated by these two powerful religious groups and refuses to perform miracles for them at their command. He calmly comments, "You hypocrites can predict the weather by the color of the sky, but you cannot discern the signs of the times." He looks at each one of them and adds, "There shall be no sign given to this wicked generation."

When Jesus turns and walks away, Simon quickly steps in between Him and the religious leaders. Although the situation is tense, I smother a laugh at the dejected looks on the faces of the Pharisees and Sadducees as some of them are scratching their heads in wonder, while others are red-faced and angrily ask, "Doesn't He know who we are?" Apparently, they do not know who Jesus is.

Before leaving Magdala, a woman with seven demons is brought to Jesus. At His command, the demons are cast out, and she instantly falls at His feet and worships Him. As Jesus and "The Twelve" walk away, she watches in awe through tears of joy. When Joseph and I pass her, she introduces herself as Mary and asks, "What must I do to be a disciple of His?"

After I tell her, "All you have to do is follow Him," she immediately joins the group without hesitation.

I am thankful to Simon and Andrew for arranging for Joseph and me to sail on the ship with Jesus and "The Twelve." Even though we must do much of the manual labor, it gives us the opportunity to be with Jesus and to see and hear Him away from the crowds. We witness His demeanor and how He interacts among those He trusts most. Plus, we are becoming closer friends with the other apostles and getting to know each of them personally.

We navigate the boat toward the shore of Bethsaida and disembark next to where Abba, Seba, Benjamin, and Daniel are busily counting their day's catch. We only get to see them occasionally when our paths cross, so we try to take every opportunity to see our families—being away from them is the hardest part of following Jesus. They are unaware of our presence until Joseph and I sneak up on them, grab our fathers around the neck, and yell, "Surprise!"

Astonished by our sudden appearance, Abba hugs me tightly, and tears cloud his eyes. "I have missed you, son. I know you are doing what is best, but you do not realize how much your mother and I have missed you."

"I have missed you, too...and Mother." I give Benjamin, Seba, and Daniel warm embraces. "And all of you, too!"

Joseph and I enthusiastically begin telling them about our recent experiences since we last saw them but are interrupted as Jesus exits the boat. He is immediately accosted by a blind man and his friends begging Jesus to restore the man's sight. Jesus takes the blind man by the hand and leads him to the edge of town. Following them are the blind man's friends, "The Twelve," Benjamin, Daniel, Seba and Joseph, Abba and me, and a few curious townspeople.

When Jesus spits on the blind man's eyes and puts His hands on him, Jesus asks, "Do you see anything now?" The blind man looks up and says, "I see men like trees, walking." Jesus puts His hands on the man's eyes again and has him look up, and this time the man excitedly proclaims, "I can see clearly now! Thank you, Jesus!"

Normally, Jesus' miracles are immediate. At first, I do not understand why it takes Him two attempts to restore this man's sight, but then it hits me. Jesus is teaching us (or me) a lesson. At first, I only physically see the miracle and am amazed at what Jesus is doing and miss its spiritual importance. But like the blind man, I do not see things clearly and comprehend their significance until I take a second glance. Maybe I am finally realizing what is happening in my life. Although I am witnessing some unbelievable fetes, I am now not only experiencing them with my eyes only, but also with my soul. Jesus smiles at me, nods his head, and winks as if He read my thoughts.

Jesus tells him to go home, and we follow the once-blind man and his friends into town. He stops and tells every person he meets about his miraculous vision even though Jesus told him not to. Joseph and I must have been preoccupied talking to our fathers, Benjamin, and Daniel because when I turn around to see what Jesus' response to the man's disobedience will be, Jesus and the apostles are not behind us. "They cannot be too far away, but where did they disappear to? Abba, I must find them. Hopefully, I will be home soon. Tell Mother I love her."

Joseph and I hurriedly retrace our footsteps to where the blind man's sight was restored. Like dogs tracking the trail of a hunted animal, we search for any sign of Jesus and the apostles. We finally catch a glimpse of them in the distance heading north toward Caesarea Philippi.

We sprint toward them, but Jesus and the remainder of the apostles pay us no attention and continue walking north while Simon back tracks to meet us to prevent us from joining the group of men. "I am sorry, fellows, but Jesus wants to be alone with the apostles to provide us with insight into our future roles in His ministry. Be ready to rejoin us on a moment's notice."

My voice shakes when I speak. "We can't go with you now?"

"Sorry, not this time. Jesus wants to avoid any distractions so He can provide the apostles with private instructions. As soon as possible, we will let you know where we are, and you can meet us there."

We exchange hugs, and Joseph and I glumly watch Simon run to catch up with Jesus and the other apostles. Joseph pats me on the shoulder and smiles. "I have been homesick lately anyway, so let's go enjoy some time with our families. We have been gone a long time, and it will be nice to be home again. Plus, we have a lot of information we need to share with them."

I am unresponsive while Joseph tries to converse with me. He soon falls silent and remains that way for the duration of our journey home. My spirits are lifted as we approach our homes and see Elizabeth, Benjamin, Daniel, his wife and baby, and our parents standing outside talking. Our pace increases. Actually, we start running to them, and I hug and kiss Mother and Abba.

It is nice to be home.

# THE WARNING

Elizabeth, Benjamin, and our parents sit silently while Joseph and I share every memorable detail of Jesus and Simon walking on the water. Daniel and his wife, Esther, almost fall off the bench in disbelief. Without interruption, everyone listens intently as we tell them about the healing of the deaf and mute man and the feeding of the crowd on the east shore.

Benjamin leans toward Joseph and touches his arm. "Is there any truth to the rumors circulating about the religious leaders being extremely upset with Jesus? Are the number of His followers really decreasing? I noticed there was hardly anyone meeting Him today. We didn't even know you were in the immediate area."

"The rumors are true. To say the Pharisees and Sadducees are extremely upset with Jesus is probably an understatement. I think they feel threatened by His authority and knowledge. They try to trap Him into doing or saying certain things, but He is always one step ahead of them and makes them look foolish. They are losing credibility with the Jews because of Him. Or so we've been told."

"The influence of the religious leaders probably has some impact on the reduction of Jesus' followers, but many of His followers became disillusioned thinking that the Messiah was going to rebel against the Roman government. That is not His message. He teaches humility, love, and forgiveness."

I provide an additional explanation. "Many of His followers also left because they misunderstood what He meant when He was teaching in the temple and said 'to eat His flesh and drink His blood to have eternal life.' They took what He said literally—and that confused many of them and scared them away."

Everyone gasps, and Abba raises his brow in shock. "I can understand why it would upset everyone. I would have probably walked away, too. Why would He say something like that? We are not cannibals. Surely, He knows we are not going to eat His flesh and drink His blood."

I am impressed at how well I remember Simon's and Andrew's explanation. "The spirit must be fed for it to mature and grow just like the physical body needs food and water to survive. We hunger and thirst for nourishment like the soul yearns for truth and guidance. Jesus' teaching and example are the sources of that nourishment. He was not promoting everyone to eat His physical body or drink His blood. He speaks many times in ways many people do not understand—He was only saying we must feed on His teaching to have eternal life."

Everyone falls silent as if to absorb and make sense of my explanation. Abba interrupts the silence. "I would not have interpreted it that way, but I can accept your explanation. Did the two of you understand what He meant?"

I laugh. "Oh, no! We were just as confused as those that walked away until Simon and Andrew explained it to us."

For several days, Joseph and I return to our old roles of fishermen and find ourselves spending much of our time sharing what we have learned from following Jesus, especially with Daniel. He is already a believer because our fathers and Benjamin have very convincingly told him everything they could remember about Jesus.

He says he would like to join us sometime, but currently, his number-one priority is the role of husband and father, especially since moving to Bethsaida. "I just can't leave them this soon after moving to a strange place. Maybe in another few months after we have become more settled, I can sneak away for a while."

Joseph offers some encouragement. "I hope you can. I know you do not want to leave your wife and child, but there are many followers who have done so. I do not think you will regret it. As Benjamin said long ago, 'God will provide for His followers.' You know you are always welcome to join us."

We receive word that we can reunite with Jesus and "the Twelve," so Joseph and I gather our belonging and hug our family members one last time before leaving. I look at Daniel. "Are you sure you don't want to come with us, Daniel?"

Daniel shakes his head. "I cannot leave my family now, Matthias. Maybe, next time."

"I want you and all the family to spend as much time with Him as you can while we have the opportunity. You never know what the future brings with the direction this country is headed."

I sense that something is different when we finally find Jesus and "the Twelve." The apostles barely speak as we approach them. They seem more distant and concerned about something and look nervously from face-to-face at those gathering around them like they have been threatened. We greet Simon and Andrew with hugs, and I ask what has happened. But Simon and Andrew shrug it off and tell us we will talk later. "Jesus is about to speak to the people who have gathered."

Even Jesus seems different. He appears more solemn and more purposeful as He begins to speak. "Whoever desires to come after Me, let him deny himself, take up his cross, and follow Me." In the Roman form of execution, condemned criminals are required to carry their own crosses through the streets to the execution site. Am I going to have to do that? I glance toward Simon and Andrew for explanation but receive none.

"For whoever desires to save his life will lose it, but whoever loses his life for My sake and the gospel's will save it." What is Jesus talking about? Are we about to die? No wonder they look so troubled.

"For what will it profit a man if he gains the whole world and loses his own soul? What will a man give in exchange for his soul? Whoever is ashamed of Me and My words in this adulterous and sinful generation, of him the Son of Man also will be ashamed when He comes in glory of His Father with the holy angels."

As the crowd disperses, I sit dumbfounded, not understanding anything that Jesus has just spoken. Joseph must feel the same way because he has not said a word. I need some answers and run to Simon and Andrew. "Please. What did Jesus mean? I am very confused."

Simon takes me by the arm and pulls me away from the crowd, followed by Andrew and Joseph. "You asked earlier what has happened—you noticed things seem different. You are very observant because they are. As a disciple of Jesus, you are owed an explanation and need to decide if you want to continue to follow Him."

"Of course, I do. Why would I not want to follow our Messiah?"

"While the apostles were alone with Jesus, He told us that He must go to Jerusalem, suffer many things from the elders, chief priests, and scribes." Andrew pauses to brush away a tear. "He said that He is going to be killed and be raised the third day."

"*What?*" Joseph and I ask simultaneously.

"Things are going to get more dangerous for the followers of Jesus. You are old enough to know what 'taking up one's cross' means.' Are you willing to do that for Jesus' and the gospel's sake?" Simon looks closely at Joseph's and my reaction.

I drop my head and stare at the ground. I cannot look at Simon in the eyes. "I – I don't know."

"Only you can make that decision." Simon grabs my shoulders and holds me tightly. "Give it some serious thought because it may come to that."

Joseph is pale, has not moved or said a word, and is staring blankly into space. Andrew puts his arm around Joseph's shoulder. "Are you alright?"

He shakes his head. "I don't know what to do. I need time to think about it."

Andrew tries to reassure us. "When the time comes, we will all do the right thing."

I am not surprised by Simon's and Andrew's response when I ask if they have made their decision. "We are continuing to follow Jesus, even unto death."

This time I look into Simon's eyes. "I don't know if I can do that, Simon. I wish I knew."

We stand in silence until Simon smiles and puffs out his chest. "Jesus blessed me and changed my name to Peter when I professed He was the Christ, the Son of the living God."

Andrew punches him. "Simon, or Peter as we need to start calling him, is being modest, too. Jesus also told him he would be 'the rock' His church would be founded upon, and he would be given the keys to the kingdom of heaven."

Some of the tension is released as we all laugh when Simon blushes—I mean Peter.

I give him a congratulatory pat on the back. "Calling you Peter is going to take getting accustomed to."

My demeanor and thoughts go back to the decision I must make. "What do you think is really going to happen? Do you think Jesus is saying that to teach us another lesson? Or do you think He knows what is about to happen?"

"Unfortunately, I believe He is predicting the future. After He told us He would be killed, I took Jesus aside and scolded Him for saying such a thing." Peter drops his head dejectedly, "He became very stern with me, told me to quote, 'get behind Me, Satan,' and was very offended by my attitude. He went on to say I was not aware of God's plan and was only thinking from a human selfish standpoint. He has never talked to me that way or in that tone of voice."

Joseph runs his fingers through his hair. "It is hard to believe with as many followers Jesus has...do you believe He would be killed?"

Andrew is quick to respond. "He has also offended many people in high positions. Some of them will stop at nothing to remove any obstacle standing in their way. After hearing how determined and authoritative Jesus spoke, I think it is only in God's hands what will happen. The only thing we can do is choose to follow Him or not. If we follow Him, we need to keep our eyes and ears open for any threats. And be ready to face any adversary. You fellows need to decide for yourselves what you want to do—we cannot make that decision for you. Whatever you decide, we understand."

Peter and Andrew rejoin "the Twelve" while Joseph and I sit in silence, wrestling with our decision. "What are you going to do, Joseph?"

"I wish Father was here to advise me because the only thing I know is I am scared. I thought I was a strong believer, but I do not know if I am committed enough to give my life for Jesus and the gospel. Have you made a decision yet?"

I shake my head no. "I know exactly how you feel. I believe with all my heart Jesus is the Messiah, but I do not want to die, either. My heart tells me to continue following Jesus, but my mind tells me otherwise."

We sit in silence, weighing our options. It seems like we have been sitting here for hours, but I am sure it has not been that long. I clear my throat and break the silence. "I know following my heart is what I should do, and I do not know if I could live with myself if I did not follow our Messiah while I have the opportunity. I guess I just made my decision. I am going to follow Him."

"Since you put it that way, I guess I did too. Are we going to tell our family about the dangers we may be facing? As believers, they may be encountering the same dangers and need to know."

"We must tell them. And the sooner, the better. Although Passover is several months away, I am sure they will be coming to Jerusalem for it, if not sooner. Jerusalem could be dangerous for all of us. They need to be cautious. We all do."

With his voice quivering, Joseph worriedly repeats, "We must tell them. We need to go home, Matthias. We must warn them as soon as possible. I know we just got here, but we need to go home."

We find Simon (I mean Peter) and Andrew standing with John and James and tell them our decision. "We decided we are going to follow Jesus, but we want to go home to warn our families before we resume our journey with Him."

Peter responds as Jesus' eyes meet mine, "Although it may be premature to warn your families, I understand your concerns. After what Jesus just told this group of followers, I do not think He would expect anything different from you."

"In fact, tell them to pass the word to our father," James adds.

Andrew echoes, "And ours, too. But tell them not to spread this around. We do not want believers to panic and start acting irrationally."

# A POSSIBLE THREAT

Abba shades his eyes from the afternoon sun and squints as we approach the boat docked at the shore. "What are you two doing home so soon?"

Joseph and I hop on board before Abba, Seba, and Daniel have time to get off the boat. I give Abba a quick hug and whisper loud enough for them to hear, but no one else. "We have some news—news that the family needs to be made aware of. Although nothing has happened yet, we, as followers of Jesus, are in danger. We are here to warn the family."

Our fathers look at us in stunned silence while we quickly relay what we heard Jesus say, what Peter and Andrew told us, and the commitment we are going to have to make if we choose to continue to be disciples of Jesus. No one speaks, but I can see the worried looks on our fathers' faces. Their brows are furrowed, and both are grimacing as if in pain.

As if he really does not want to know, Abba takes a deep breath and swallows hard. "Have you decided what you are going to do yet?"

He hesitates as Joseph and I both nod our heads.

"Well, you are not going back, are you?"

I speak for both of us, "We are following Jesus."

Seba grabs Joseph's arm. "You can't. It is too dangerous for you."

Joseph hugs Seba tightly then pulls away to look into his worried eyes. "I...we appreciate and understand why you are concerned. Matthias and I are, too. That is why we are here now. Although we do not know what hazards we may be facing, we are ready to meet them head-on. Who knows—we may not be facing anything worth worrying about."

I am impressed with Joseph's response and attitude. I could not have said it any better myself.

Abba puts his trembling hands on my shoulders and holds me at arms' length. Tears are in his eyes. "Son, I can't lose you." He shakes his head back and forth. "I know following Jesus is important to the two of you. It is important that we all believe in Him. But possibly dying for Him? That is a whole different situation."

It is difficult for me to hold back the tears when I see his concern. My voice cracks when I speak. "Abba. I do not mean to disrespect you in any way, but we came here to warn you...not to get your permission. We have had time to consider all the consequences, and yes, they could be very unpleasant. We are prepared to take that chance. We cannot desert our Messiah."

He pulls me close and does not let go. With his arm tightly around my shoulder, we silently walk home. Abba's reaction to the news is nothing compared to Mother's. Before I can tell her what Joseph and I have decided, tears are streaming down her cheeks, and she screams hysterically. "NOOOOO! You can't go back!"

After telling her Joseph and I are going to continue following Jesus despite the consequences, Mother vehemently shakes her head and repeatedly screams, "NO!"

I try to hug her, but she pushes me away. Mother brushes the tears away, but they are immediately replaced with more. Through deep sobs, she finally speaks. "Although I am not happy with your decision, Matthias...you are a grown man. Believe me...I would stop you...if I could." Her body is shaking as she hugs me, turns, and walks away crying.

Through the blur of tears in my eyes, I walk out the door. I must get some fresh air. I cannot bear to see the panged look on her face any longer as she paces back and forth, wringing her trembling hands. Other than losing Arat and the baby, telling my parents that I am choosing possible death following the Messiah over staying safe with them is the worst thing I have ever faced. Am I doing the right thing?

Martha brushes past me and enters the house without speaking. Her eyes are already swollen and red. I follow her inside, and she heads directly to Mother. They fall into each other's arms, sobbing on each other's shoulders. Abba looks lost as he watches them at a distance, not knowing what to do.

I walk back outside. Seba pulls me close when I exit the door and whispers in my ear. "We heard Rachel and know telling her did not go well. Martha's not happy about it, but it sounds like she took the news somewhat better."

He gently pats me on the shoulder and glances at Joseph. "Give them some time, and maybe they will be more supportive. It is difficult for all of us." Tears fill his eyes and roll down his cheeks. "As parents, and especially for your mothers, it is hard to accept your one and only child could be killed because of his beliefs."

Daniel follows Benjamin and Elizabeth across the courtyard toward us. Elizabeth squeezes my hand. "While Daniel was updating us, we heard the screams. How is Rachel?"

"Martha and Abba are with her now. She and Martha are in there bawling." I look toward the open door. "I had to get out for a little while."

Before entering the house, Elizabeth gives me a reassuring hug. "She will always be worried about your safety. We all will be. But knowing how dedicated you are to the cause, I am certain she will eventually proudly accept and respect your decision."

Benjamin grabs my shoulders and turns me, so I am looking directly into his eyes. "Don't second-guess yourselves. You boys are making the correct decision. Be strong and continue the path you are on because Jesus is our Messiah."

"I knew I could count on you, Benjamin. After what the two of us saw in Jesus' early ministry, I knew you would understand. You would do the same thing if you had not chosen to stay here so Joseph and I could follow Jesus. Thank you for that." With tears streaming down my face into my beard, I hug Benjamin tightly and sob on his shoulder. At least we have the full support of one family member.

After seeing my mother's agonized face every time I close my eyes and the remainder of the night filled with nightmares, I tiredly join Abba, Seba, Benjamin, Daniel, and Joseph for a day of fishing from the shore. Last night is the first time in months, I have had a nightmare. God, please do not let them return. Everyone is melancholy and unusually quiet, knowing tomorrow Joseph and I will be leaving to rejoin Jesus and His followers.

While everyone else goes home, Joseph and I stop by the dock as promised to privately warn Zebedee and Jonah of the possible dangers facing believers in the Messiah. Zebedee thunders. "James and John won't give up easily."

I place my forefinger up to my mouth to quiet him. "They want to keep this confidential to prevent believers from acting erratically. Do not tell anyone."

"I hope it does not come to a battle, but I know Simon and Andrew will fight to the end if they think they have to. And they know how to protect themselves and are not afraid to do so." Jonah tugs at his sash as if unsheathing a sword.

I had forgotten about Peter having the sword until now. Does Andrew have one, too? Joseph and I always carry our fishing knives with us, but is that enough to protect ourselves? Although I have never used one, should we be carrying swords, too?

# A SECRET IS TOLD

Although our mothers now support our decision, I do not feel they are totally convinced we are making the correct choice. Especially mine. But at least we do have their blessings. My heart breaks as Joseph and I walk away. Not only am I crying, but so is everyone else. Mother is on her knees sobbing like a child, while Abba kneels by her side. Martha is leaning upon Seba for support. Benjamin is usually stoic and does not show his emotions, but he even has tears running down his cheeks as he hugs Elizabeth. Daniel and Esther are in tears but manage a smile as they wave goodbye.

Before topping the hill, I look back at my family one last time. No one has moved. They return my wave when I wave at them, and I am overcome with emotion. This is a sight I will not forget. I sit on a downed tree and cry like a baby when I know they can no longer see me. Am I making the correct decision? I do not know anymore.

Joseph rests a consoling hand on my shoulder and does not say anything for a while—he just lets me cry. After a while, he pats my shoulder. "Matthias, we need to get moving. We can't stay here."

We plod slowly and silently along the path to Capernaum. Leaving my family in their sorrowful state keeps replaying in my head and makes the journey seem to last forever, even though it is not extremely far. We go directly to Peter's house, and I am glad to see he is standing outside. He apparently sees the grief on our faces and greets us with a comforting embrace. We tell him about our family's reaction to the threat of following Jesus, and he is pleased to know his parents have also been warned of the possible danger of being a believer.

When Joseph walks across the courtyard to visit Andrew, Peter quickly changes the subject. "I have not told anyone this, not even Andrew. I am afraid he might tell the other apostles, and Jesus told us to not tell anyone. But I must tell someone. You must promise to tell no one what I am about to say. Not even Joseph."

"I'm good at keeping secrets. But if it is this hard for you—"

Before I can finish my sentence, Peter begins, "While you were away, Jesus took James, John, and me to Mount Tabor to pray. The three of us fell asleep while Jesus was praying, and when we awoke, I had to shield my eyes because Jesus' face was glowing like the sun and His clothes were as white as snow. Two men were talking to Him, and I know you are not going to believe me when I tell you who they were."

He pauses and waits for me to ask the obvious question, "Who was it?"

"It was Moses and Elijah. Jesus called them by name...like they were old friends of His."

I do a double-take, "Moses, who led our ancestors to the Promised Land? And Elijah the prophet? Where did they come from?"

"Yes, that Moses and Elijah. They arrived after we went to sleep, but they were talking to Jesus about His demise, which is going to be fulfilled at Jerusalem."

"His death? What did they tell Him?"

Peter blushes. "I wish I knew more details, but that is all we heard." He looks away, embarrassed, and rubs his neck. "We slept through their entire conversation."

"What happened then, rosy cheeks?"

When we stop laughing, he continues, "Not sure of what to do or say, I told Jesus we could make a tabernacle for each of them if He wished. A cloud came and overshadowed the three of them, and a voice thundered from the cloud—like at Jesus' baptism. The voice declared, 'This is my beloved Son, in whom I am well pleased. Hear Him.'"

"James, John, and I were so scared we fell with our faces to the ground. Jesus touched us and said to not be afraid. And when we looked up, Jesus was standing there alone."

"Where did...Moses and Elijah go?"

Peter shrugs his shoulders. "I don't know...one moment they were there, and the next they were gone. They disappeared with the cloud. Truly, Jesus is the Son of God. I should not have told you this, but I had to tell someone. As we were descending the mount, Jesus commanded us to tell no one until the Son of Man is risen from the dead—whatever that means."

With that recount of events by Peter, I am reassured I am making the correct decision to continue as a disciple of Christ. I repeat Peter's statement, "Truly, He is the Son of God."

Peter immediately changes the subject when Andrew and Joseph stroll over and sit. "Jesus called the apostles a 'faithless generation' after we were unable to heal a possessed boy. After He healed the lad, Jesus reiterated the Son of Man is about to be betrayed, killed, and the third day be raised up.

"I am trying to understand." I look off into space, not focusing on anything in particular. "Did He say when all this is supposed to happen?"

"No, but He is preparing us for it. This is the second time He has warned us. It must be soon, though, and two of the biggest Jewish festivals in Jerusalem are upcoming—Sukkot and Passover. We need to be ready for anything."

Joseph stands, then sits back down. "How can we prepare for something we don't know what we are dealing with? or when it is going to happen?

Andrew scratches his beard. "Stay alert. Keep your eyes and ears open to any threats and stay together."

Peter adds, "And keep your knives with you at all times—you may need them."

I have never used my knife as a weapon. Will I be able to if I am confronted?

# GOING TO A FESTIVAL

Sukkot, the Feast of Tabernacles celebrating completion of the wheat harvest, is rapidly approaching. Jesus continues to teach in Galilee instead of preparing to go to Jerusalem for the celebration. Because Jesus had healed a man on the Sabbath, rumors are rampant the Pharisees, and many of the Jews in Judea and especially Jerusalem want to kill Him. With His brothers knowing this, I do not understand their logic. Almost mocking Him, they try to convince Him He should go to Jerusalem for the Feast and to show Himself to the world so it can see His good works.

His brother Judah taunts Him, "How do You expect people to know who You are if You stay here? No one does anything in secret when he seeks to be known openly."

James, another brother, chimes in, "You do these miraculous fetes and need to demonstrate Your extraordinary powers for all to see. You need an audience. What better place is there than the Feast of Tabernacles in Jerusalem?"

Judah, James, and His two other brothers turn sharply and leave to begin their journey to the Feast after Jesus calmly replies, "You go up to the Feast. I am not going yet because My time has not come."

Do they want Him killed, too? They remind me of the eleven brothers of Joseph, son of Jacob and Rachel from our ancestry, who sold him into slavery because they were jealous of the attention their father gave him. And what does He mean that His "time has not come"? Is He talking about His death?

Jesus eventually decides to attend the week-long Feast, so "The Twelve" and a few of us disciples make the trek to Jerusalem. Is it safe for us to go there? I recollect Peter saying that Moses and Elias had talked to Jesus about His decease in Jerusalem. Will it be this trip? I have my knife handy, but am I ready to use it if we are threatened?

Upon our arrival, the vast number of booths or tabernacles lining the streets and in the gardens remind us of the temporary dwellings our Jewish ancestry constructed in the desert after the Exodus from slavery in Egypt. As we construct our own tents for the festival, the children of God remember His faithfulness to our forefathers in the wilderness. Since this is one of the most popular festivals, people happily crowd the streets and are also observing the completion of the wheat harvest.

Jesus, having been a carpenter, and James and John quickly construct their sukkah. Jesus watches Peter, Andrew, Joseph, and me as we struggle with our booth and laughs. He grabs some of the tree branches and palm fronds and begins covering the roof as the Torah directs. "It is a good thing our ancestors did not have to wait for you four to build your booth every day, or our people would have never made it to the Promised Land."

With some of the leftover palm, myrtle, and willow branches, we each form our lulav to wave at the festival ceremonies. The cluster of branches is a reminder of how Yahweh was with our ancestors' regardless of where they were—palms in the valleys, myrtles in the mountains. Even in the desert, He provided water for them, which is symbolized by the willow branch. The completion of our ancestors' journey to the Promised Land is represented by carrying an etrog, a yellow citrus fruit, which we pull from a nearby tree.

At least it is a cool autumn day. With the hood of His robe covering His head and much of His face, Jesus moves undetected through the masses. John, James, Andrew, and Peter surround Him for protection. The remainder of "The Twelve" and the few disciples follow behind but are spread far enough apart to avoid undue attention to Him.

Jesus loses His anonymity, though, when He decides to teach in the temple mid-week of the Festival. "The Twelve" and His disciples eye the crowd and listen for any comments or watch for potential danger. I hear whispers in the audience about His vast knowledge, but they are too afraid to speak openly for fear of being banished from the synagogues by the Pharisees. Others openly accuse Him of having a demon and want to kill Him. Even the Pharisees and chief priests send officers to take Him. We, the apostles and disciples, crowd closer together when we hear these accusations and threats. I look at Peter and hope no one else notices—he has his hand on the hilt of his sword and looks like he is ready to use it. I do not know how He does it, but Jesus manages to escape the crowd without being captured.

The final day of the Feast comes. We reverently watch as the priests carrying golden pitchers of water march in solemn procession from the Pool of Siloam into the temple. They pour out the water in commemoration of the water Yahweh had provided to our ancestors in the desert. The ritual reminds us of the prophecies concerning the coming of God's Spirit upon His people.

Everyone turns and stares as Jesus suddenly stands and cries out, "If anyone thirsts, let him come to Me and drink. He who believes in Me, as the Scripture has said, out of his heart will flow rivers of living water."

Oh, no! After the way the crowd reacted the other day, how are they going to respond to Jesus claiming to be the Messiah, especially in the middle of this holy ritual?

It goes surprisingly well, though. Many in the crowd say that He is the Prophet and others say He is the Christ. Of course, there is some division among the spectators, and some want to seize Him. But no one lays a hand on Him as He walks through their midst and goes to the Mount of Olives to pray.

Early the next morning, Jesus returns to the Temple. It is the last day of the sacred year—the Eighth Day of Assembly or Shemini Atzeret. The Twelve survey the crowd for any threats.

When He sits to teach, Jesus waits while curious onlookers and others who want to absorb His every word gather around Him.

But before He can get started, here come the scribes and Pharisees to try and trap Him again. They are pulling a woman who is struggling to get away, and she tries to break her fall and slides on the gravel when they sling her to the ground at the feet of Jesus. With hands bleeding, she cowers before Him and the group of men.

"This woman was taken in the very act of adultery. Moses commanded in the Law that she should be stoned. What do you say about that, Jesus?" It is strange that they did not arrest the man, too, since that is what the Law requires.

As if He did not hear them, Jesus squats and starts writing in the sand with His finger. Some of the men are already gathering rocks to stone her while awaiting His answer while the remainder crane and stretch their necks to see what Jesus is doing in the sand. The woman shudders in fear. The men are persistent and keep demanding an answer to their question. When Jesus stands, I catch a glimpse of what He has written—it is a list of names.

He looks into each of their faces before answering them. "He that is without sin, let him cast the first stone at her." He kneels and continues writing in the sand. I guess those charging her see their names in the sand and have guilty consciences, because they gradually drop the rocks and leave one-by-one.

Again, Jesus has humiliated the scribes and Pharisees in front of a large crowd. I cannot help but feel the tension is only going to get worse between Jesus and the Pharisees. The Pharisees are not going to give up, and Jesus is not going to back down.

After the last of the ones condemning the woman walks away, Jesus puts His hand on her hand. "Neither do I condemn you. Go and sin no more."

The woman was trembling in fear before but is now giddy with joy. She brushes the hair away from her face with the back of her hand and smiles at Jesus. "Thank you for defending me from that mob. My life will be forever changed because of You."

As she walks away, Jesus sits and continues teaching the crowd. Some of the crowd get riled when Jesus proclaims His divinity, "Before Abraham was, I am." Some people mimic the religious leaders and pick up rocks to stone Him for blasphemy, but again, Jesus walks through the midst of them without being harmed.

On the Sabbath, we pass by a blind man sitting by the street. Someone said he had been blind since birth. One of the apostles asks, "Master, who sinned? This man or his parents that he was born blind?"

Most Jews believe pain and suffering are the results of some great sin committed by the victim or an ancestor. I felt that guilt after the deaths of Arat and our son and wondered what I had done to cause them. I had not thought about experiencing that guilt until now. But since Jesus hugged me when we first met face-to-face, I am thankful I have not felt that way since.

Jesus looks at the blind man before answering. "Neither. He was born this way, so the works of God should be made known in him. I must do that work while I am still here. While I am in the world, I am the light of the world."

Jesus spits on the ground, makes clay of the spittle, and anoints the eyes of the blind man with the clay. "Go and wash in the pool of Siloam." An on-looker leads the man to the pool, as Jesus said.

Several days pass, and Jesus goes searching for the once-blind man after hearing he was excommunicated from the synagogue. Once found, the man discloses he was brought before the Pharisees, who questioned him about who and how he received his sight.

"After I told them what happened, some of the Pharisees proclaimed the Man who healed me could not be from God since He performed the deed on the Sabbath. A man sent from God would know that is prohibited by the Law. Others asked how a man who is a sinner performs such an act. I was asked who I thought the Healer was. My answer was a prophet."

"Some of the Pharisees did not even believe I had ever been blind. Especially blind since birth. They called for my parents and asked if I was their son and how long had I been blind. When they told them I had been blind my entire life, the Pharisees asked them how I received my sight. My parents were frustrated with the questioning and answered, 'We were not there. He is of age so ask him.'"

"Being annoyed by all the repeated questions, I told them if this Man is not from God, He could do nothing. The Pharisees responded I was born in sin and asked who I thought I was trying to teach them about the ways of God. With that said, they cast me out of the synagogue. I can never go back in there."

Jesus lets out a heavy sigh and looks into the once blind eyes. "Do you believe in the Son of God?"

"Who is He Lord, so I may believe in Him?"

"It is He who is talking with you."

The man kneels at Jesus' feet. "I believe...I believe! You gave me sight. How could I not believe?"

A man born blind now sees and knows He is the Messiah. What is it going to take for the Pharisees who have been teaching us about the coming Messiah to recognize Him? Why are they blind to the fact?

Even though Jesus knows the religious leaders in the area want to kill him, we leave Jerusalem but remain in Judea. I do not know if it is such a good idea. I certainly do not feel safe here.

# TWO BY TWO

I am excited when Jesus chooses Joseph and me as two of the seventy followers for His next mission—to go in pairs to area villages, preparing them for His upcoming visits. When Jesus says He is sending us "as lambs among wolves," I get a sick feeling in my stomach and look to see if Joseph looks uneasy, too. He does not seem to be alarmed. At least Jesus is pairing us so we can provide moral and physical support for whatever challenges we may face.

We all sit while Jesus gives us specific instructions. We are not to carry a money bag, extra clothing, or sandals because provisions will be the laborer's reward. And we are not to greet anyone along the road since that will delay us from our task. Once we find a family to stay with, we are to remain there and not go from house to house. I understand His reasoning. Not only would the initial host be offended if we left his home to go to another, but it could also cause conflict and jealously between neighbors, especially if we did not stay with each one of them. Plus, staying in one place provides a base for us to complete the assigned task while there. I am anxious to try it when He tells us He is giving us the power to heal their sick.

Jesus tells Joseph and me to go toward Bethany, which is only a few miles away. The apostles are staying with Jesus while we are gone, so Peter and Andrew agree to keep our belongings since we cannot carry them with us. We bid farewell and begin the short walk.

We ascend the eastern slope of the Mount of Olives to a small village. Not sure of where to go, we stand in the street in front of a small house. Almost immediately, a young man about our age comes to us. I greet him as Jesus instructed. "Peace be to this house."

"Shalom. Welcome to my home. I am Nathan."

A young attractive woman exits the house. "This is my wife, Golda. Please stay with us."

As we enter the house, a young child cries, and Golda rushes to him. Nathan waits for Golda to get out of hearing range and leans toward us so we can hear him. "That is our son, Levi. He is four years old and has never been able to use his legs."

"My name is Matthias, and this is my cousin Joseph. We have been sent by the Messiah to announce His arrival to your village. He will be coming here soon."

Nathan shows no enthusiasm or excitement—in fact, he shows no emotion at all. I hope Joseph is thinking the same thing as I glance at him. He gives me a little nod as if he is reading my mind. "We have never done this before, but bring your son to us. The Messiah gave us power to heal the sick. We will try to heal him."

With a smirk on his face, Nathan stands motionless with his arms crossed. No one speaks until Golda reenters the room carrying Levi. Levi is small for his age but looks healthy. If Golda was not carrying him, one would not know there was anything wrong. His black hair hangs to his shoulders in ringlets. And he stares at Joseph and me curiously with large, brown eyes.

Nathan suddenly waves his hand as if dismissing the possibility we can heal his son. "These two men say the Messiah is coming to Bethany, and they have been given powers by Him to cure our son." The sarcasm in his voice leaves no doubt in my mind he does not believe us.

He assumes a confrontational stance with his arms crossed and jaws clenched. "Do your magic. I will not believe it until I see it."

Joseph and I squat down beside Levi as Golda lays him on the ground. Levi glances from Joseph to me and squirms as close to Golda as he can. "We are not going to hurt you. We are here to help you."

Not knowing exactly what to do, I say a silent prayer, "Father, so that You may be glorified, please hear our request."

I put my hand on Levi's lifeless left leg, and Joseph puts his hand on the right one. Joseph and I lift our other hand toward heaven and speak simultaneously and in unison as if we had planned it. "Father, heal this child."

Joseph and I quickly jerk our hands away when we feel motion in Levi's legs. Golda and Nathan both gasp as Levi moves both legs and tries to stand. He is a little wobbly at first, but his eyes twinkle, and he giggles as he stands for the first time in his life. Golda bursts into tears of joy. Nathan is not ashamed of his tears either. They both grab Levi and squeeze him tightly.

They fall on their knees and begin to bow before Joseph and me. "No. No. Stand up. We are only messengers of the Messiah. Do not worship us. Worship the One that sent us."

By this time, Levi is ready to play and runs through the open door. Golda is one step behind him and yells loud enough for all her neighbors to hear. "He's been healed! Levi can walk! God healed him!"

"Thank you! Thank you! Thank you! I am so sorry for not believing you." Tears are rolling down Nathan's cheeks. "I apologize for my earlier behavior." Nathan squeezes tightly as he hugs Joseph and me. "Please forgive me."

Joseph pulls away to look Nathan in the eyes. "We did not do it. God did. Thank Him."

We all walk outside and see Levi and Golda surrounded by their neighbors. "Here is our first audience, Joseph. It is time for us to do what we were sent here to do."

As Jesus instructed, we begin, "The kingdom of God is come nigh unto you. The Messiah will soon visit your community. We are only His messengers to alert you of His coming."

The crowds listening to us grow each day, including an increase in the number of "wolves," as Jesus called them. Joseph and I know many are enthusiastic about meeting the Messiah, especially those who we have healed of their infirmities. However, some are remaining silent and non-committal with the increase in the number of Pharisees coming to hear what we say and inciting hecklers and encouraging threats against us.

From the direction of the Pharisees, a rock sails past my face and barely misses Joseph's head. We quickly finish speaking and are walking back to Nathan's house when Joseph stops me in my tracks. "I think it is time for us to leave while we can."

"I agree. It is getting more hostile each day. The next rock thrown at us might connect with one of our heads." I punch Joseph in the arm and laugh. "Of course, it would just bounce off yours."

We hug Nathan and Golda, thank them for their hospitality, and return to where we left Jesus and "the Twelve." We are not the only ones. It looks like all seventy of us are arriving at the camp at the same time. We begin sharing our experiences but soon realize everyone's story is basically the same. One of the seventy summarizes everyone's experience in one sentence—even the devils were subject to us through Your name.

# RAISING THE DEAD

We cross the Jordan where John the Baptist first baptized and into Perea. Since travel is difficult and unpleasant due to the cold rainy winter, Jesus remains there to minister to the public and has many new believers.

Spring arrives, and drier weather sets in. Pink buds begin to form on the almond trees and soon turn into sweet-smelling blossoms. The other fruit trees soon burst into bloom, and leaves form on all the trees. Wildflowers dot the hillsides.

A boy who looks to be in his early teens approaches Jesus. "Master, the sisters of your friend Lazarus want you to know he is critically sick and about to die. They want you to come to his aid immediately."

Jesus looks undaunted, sits on a large rock, and closes His eyes. "This sickness will not end in death, but for the glory of God so the Son of God may be glorified by it."

The boy rocks from one foot to the other while staring at Jesus. Jesus remains motionless. The teen glances around at us as if looking for advice, but we are all as unsure of what to do as he is. Finally, the boy shrugs his shoulders and runs off in the direction from which he came.

After two days, we begin our journey to Bethany in Judea, where Lazarus lives along with his sisters Mary and Martha. I do not know why He has waited this long, but Jesus has finally decided to go see about His friend.

Peter steps in front of Jesus, so they are face-to-face. "The Jews want to kill you, Master. Why do you want to take the chance of going back there?"

"Our friend Lazarus sleeps, and I must go to wake him."

"Sleep is good for him, Master. He must be feeling better."

"You do not understand. Lazarus is dead. I am glad for your sakes I was not there, so you will believe. We must go to him."

Shivers run up my spine when I hear Thomas, one of "The Twelve," whisper to Peter, "If Jesus is going to be killed, then let us go so we may die with Him." Joseph and I exchange worried glances but do not comment.

Near the village, a woman wearing sackcloth meets us on the road and stops in front of Jesus. "Lord, if You had been here, our brother would not be dead. I know even now, whatever You ask of God, God will give it to You."

"Martha, your brother will rise again."

"I know he will rise on the day of resurrection."

"I am the resurrection and the life. Whoever believes in Me, though he were dead, yet shall he live. Whoever lives and believes in Me will never die. Do you believe this?"

"Yes, Lord. I believe you are the Christ, the Son of God."

When Jesus asks for her sister Mary, Martha turns and runs away. Jesus does not follow her. In fact, He remains standing in the spot where she left Him until Martha returns with another woman dressed in sackcloth, followed by a group of mourners.

This bereaved woman falls at the feet of Jesus, sobbing inconsolably. Her eyes are red and swollen from crying. "If only... You had been here... Lazarus would be...alive."

Jesus looks into the face of each of the mourners and then compassionately at the grief-stricken woman at His feet. He kneels beside her. "Mary, where is he laid?"

"Come...and see." Mary begins to lead the procession. But before they can walk away, Jesus is overcome with grief and begins to weep. When they see Him crying, some of the mourners comment about how much He must have loved His friend. Others question why He had not arrived sooner when told of Lazarus' illness and healed Lazarus since He was able to heal others.

On the outskirts of Bethany, we descend the steep, uneven steps carved out of the rocky slope to the cave where Lazarus' body was placed. Jesus points to the large stone sealing the tomb. "Take away the stone."

I stifle a laugh at Martha's response. "Lord, he has been dead four days. He stinks by now."

"Did not I say you would see the glory of God? Now take away the stone."

Several of the disciples roll the stone away from the tomb's entrance while the rest of us cover our noses, awaiting the stench of death. Jesus raises His arms and looks to the sky. "Father, thank you for hearing Me. You always do. Answer My prayer, so these watching will believe You have sent Me."

When He is finished praying, He stands and cries out with a loud voice, "Lazarus, come forth!"

There is movement inside the tomb, and a shadow appears in the opening. As the figure slowly exits the tomb into the sunlight, it is the body of a man wearing the white linen cloth of the dead and the face bound with a napkin. Some in the crowd scream and run away in fear or hide behind the person in front of them. Many stand frozen in awe or clap with joy. A few faint. Believers fall on their knees praising God. Mary and Martha burst into tears of joy and bow before Jesus, thanking Him for this miracle.

Jesus looks down at them and then at Lazarus. "Loose him and let him go."

Mary and Martha run to Lazarus and cautiously remove the cloth from his face. To everyone's surprise, his skin coloring is a normal tone and not that of a man who has been dead for four days. And there is no discoloration or decay. He looks perfectly normal.

When his sisters see his condition, they latch onto him. "We never thought we would ever see you again."

His eyes well up with tears as he looks at them and smiles. Although still wrapped in the grave cloths, Lazarus holds his sisters tightly as they cling to him. "As nice as it was to be in Paradise, I am thankful to be reunited with the two of you again."

The reunion of the once dead man with his now ecstatic sisters is a very moving experience to witness for almost everyone there. However, several people walk away, and I hear one say, "I can't wait to tell the Pharisees about this and to see what their reaction will be."

As the strips of cloth encasing the once dead man are removed, I offer him one of my robes I have been carrying. He takes it from my trembling hands, thanks me, and looks past me at Jesus. Once robed, he walks to Jesus and hugs Him. They whisper softly to each other, but I cannot understand what they are saying even though I am standing close by. They hurriedly walk arm-in-arm to the house, followed closely by Mary and Martha. Once inside, the door closes behind them, leaving everyone else still amazed by the miracle we just witnessed.

Like most Jews, I believe the soul hovers above the dead body for three days hoping to reenter it, and on the fourth day, it departs to where it spends eternity with no chance of returning. Jesus just reunited a departed soul on the fourth day and has given life to a dead body—a living, breathing human being. How can people not believe He is our Messiah?

Jesus is warned by one of His believers from Jerusalem. "After hearing You raised Lazarus from the grave, the Pharisees and chief priests called a meeting with the Sanhedrin and are plotting to kill You. They believe if they continue to let You perform miracles and teach, then everyone will believe in You, and the Romans will come and take away both their temple and nation. Especially if the Jews decide to revolt. Ridding themselves of You is their only solution. They believe it would be better for one man to die instead of the nation being destroyed, so they are wanting to put an end to You—as quickly as possible."

Heeding the warning, Jesus leaves Judea, and we ascend the hills to a village called Ephraim. From here, we can overlook the plains of Jericho and the Dead Sea. At least for the moment, I feel safer knowing I am somewhat close to my relatives in Jericho.

# JOURNEY TO JERUSALEM

We leave the safety of Ephraim to join the pilgrimage of the Jews attending the Passover in Jerusalem. Jesus takes the apostles aside to talk privately, and when Jesus finishes talking to them, Peter and Andrew immediately motion for Joseph and me to come to them.

Because of the sad, dejected looks on their faces, Joseph and I run to where they are. Before we can ask what is wrong, Andrew begins talking. "Jesus just warned us for the third time that He is going to be killed."

Peter has tears in his eyes. "It is going to happen while we are in Jerusalem at the Passover."

"At the Passover? We aren't still going there, are we?"

"Yes, we are, Matthias. So be prepared. Jesus said He is going to be mocked, insulted, spit upon, scourged, and crucified. And He will rise again on the third day."

I hold my hand up to stop Peter. "Yet He still wants to make this trip? Why? I don't understand."

"Neither do we, Matthias. But He is determined to go to Jerusalem and says it is God's will."

Peter and Andrew rejoin "The Twelve" while Joseph and I follow in their footsteps through the streets of Jericho. I am staring blankly ahead, and my thoughts are racing. If Jesus is going to die, am I going to die, too? I do not want to die. Will I get to see my parents again? They usually come to the Passover, so maybe they will be in Jerusalem. What if it is not safe for them? Maybe they should not come. I need to warn them. Will I face the danger if confronted, or will I run from it? I am not a fighter, but I am no coward either. Or am I?

My thoughts are interrupted by the shouts of a blind man sitting beside the road. "Jesus, Son of David, have mercy on me!"

Some of those with him try to quiet him, but the blind man is persistent and shouts again. "Son of David, have mercy on me!"

Jesus stands still and beckons for the blind man to come to Him. The blind man casts aside his garment and is led to Jesus.

"What do you want Me to do for you?"

The blind man turns his head toward the voice. "Lord, that I may receive my sight."

"Receive your sight. Your faith has made you whole."

His sight is immediately restored, and he turns in a circle taking in all the things he has never seen. He begins thanking and praising God and gets his robe that he had cast aside, puts it on, and runs to Jesus. "Thank you, Master. I am Bartimaeus. I have nothing to make me stay here. What must I do to follow You?"

I am unable to hear Jesus' answer, but Bartimaeus closely follows Jesus as we exit Jericho.

As we enter a village on the border between Samaria and Galilee, a group of men stand isolated outside the gate—obviously, they are lepers in various stages of the disease. Some are disfigured from the blistering and oozing sores and scaly red splotches. Others have twisted limbs and can barely move. Some are missing fingers and toes. Their shaggy hair and torn dirty clothes make them even more haunting. It is difficult to look directly at them.

They cry out for help, "Jesus, Master, have pity on us!"

Those that can back away to prevent spreading the disease as Jesus takes a step toward them. Jesus has a panged look on His face as if He is suffering their pain but reaches out His hands and speaks in a comforting tone. "Go, show yourselves to the priests so you can be declared clean."

They look at Him curiously since their appearance has not changed but obey when Jesus points for them to go. They hurry away, but after a short distance, one of them returns and throws himself at Jesus' feet to thank Him. He is a Samaritan.

Jesus looks at him, gives a heavy sigh, and shakes His head—obviously disappointed he is the only one. "Were not all ten cleansed?

Where are the other nine? Has no one returned to give praise to God except this foreigner?"

The other nine are out of sight by now. He tells the healed leper to get up because his faith has made him well. When the healed man departs in the direction of the other lepers, I wonder if leprosy has returned to the ungrateful nine.

Six days before the Passover, Jesus returns to Bethany to visit Mary, Martha, and Lazarus. Since I gave Lazarus my robe and he wants to thank me for my gesture, I am asked to join them for supper. "The Twelve" are also invited.

Lazarus gives Jesus a warm embrace and thanks Him again for raising him from the dead, and washes the feet of each guest entering the house. As he washes my feet, I want to ask him what Paradise was like—but that would not be appropriate at this time. Maybe I will have the opportunity to ask him later in the evening.

Mary, the mother of Jesus, is helping the sisters plate the food... until she sees Jesus. She runs to Him and throws her arms around His neck, and kisses Him on the cheek. Overcome with emotions, she bursts into tears, and He leads her to a corner where they can talk privately. When they rejoin the group, she seems fine, so I assume they are tears of joy at seeing her son.

It has been a long time since I had a home-cooked meal, and Mary and Martha serve a feast. We have a light conversation while eating the fish stew, cheese, bread with honey, lentils, olives, and dates. The two sisters keep refilling my bowl with stew and giving me bread until I can eat no more.

After the meal, Martha brings out a pound of spikenard, a very expensive ointment normally used to anoint kings. We all silently watch Martha slowly apply the soothing ointment to Jesus' feet and then wipes them clean with her hair. The sweet odor fills the room. It is very moving to see the reverence and love she has for Jesus.

Judas Iscariot breaks the silence of this tender moment. "Why wasn't this ointment sold and given to the poor? It could have been sold for three hundred pence."

I understand his reasoning because the ointment is worth a year's wages. It could go a long way to helping those in need. Jesus does not look up but continues to watch Martha. "Leave her alone. She has kept this for the day of my burial. The poor will be with you always, but Me... I will not." Judas strolls outside, shaking his head.

As I leave the house, a crowd is gathered outside. Joseph immediately finds Peter, Andrew, and me. "Many have come because they are curious and want to see if Lazarus is really alive. But I overheard some others say the chief priests have already consulted about also putting Lazarus to death to squash the rumors of his resurrection. Lazarus may not be safe here. What should we do?"

"Thank you for the warning. I will tell Jesus." Andrew runs back into the house to relay the message.

# CHILDHOOD SECRETS

Other than the supper at Lazarus' home, I have not been around Mary, the mother of Jesus, much since she is usually with the other women following Him...until now. She is traveling with us to Jerusalem and has barely left Jesus' side since we left the home of Lazarus, Mary, and Martha. She and Jesus come to warm themselves by the fire Peter has built and sit on a boulder watching the orange flames dance before them.

The fire hisses, and the glowing ashes flurry skyward as Peter throws on another limb. "Mary, when did you realize Jesus was special?"

"Before He was ever born. It is a long story, Peter, but needs to be told." She looks at Jesus, and He nods His head for her to proceed.

"When I was pledged to be married to Joseph, one night, an angel suddenly appeared before me. Of course, it scared me. The angel told me to not be afraid—I had found favor with God and was pregnant with a son. I was to name him Jesus. Jesus would be great and called the Son of the Most High, would be given the throne of his ancestor David, and would reign over His kingdom forever. I shook my head in disbelief. How could I be pregnant since I was a virgin?"

"How did you get pregnant?" Peter blurts out and then blushes when he realizes what he just asked. "I am sorry. That came out before I thought."

Mary laughs at the red-faced fisherman. "The angel explained it this way. The Holy Spirit would come upon me, and the power of the Most High would overshadow me so the Holy One would be known as the Son of God."

Peter runs his hand through his hair and looks at Jesus, "So Joseph was not your real father?"

"Correct. Yahweh is my father. Joseph was my earthly father—and an exceptionally good one."

For a brief moment, we all sit quietly. Jesus watches Mary as she stares blankly at the fire and wipes away a tear trickling down her cheek. "Peter, it is still hard for me to believe sometimes, and I am the one who experienced it. But let me continue. I must have looked confused at the time, and the angel told me my older cousin Elisabeth was having a baby. Since she had never been able to have children when she was younger and was well past the normal age to bear children, nothing is impossible with God."

"Although a little reluctant, I told the angel that as a servant of God, may it happen to me as he had said. The angel disappeared from my sight before I could ask any questions. I wanted to ask how I was going to convince my family and especially my future husband that I had not been unfaithful to him, but I did not get the chance."

"Still dazed and confused the next morning, I left my parents' house and set out to the hill country of Judah where Elisabeth lived. I knew everything was going to be fine when I greeted her and the baby in her womb leaped." Mary looks at me. "If you did not already know, that baby was John the Baptist."

I quickly turn toward Jesus. "That is how he knew who You were when he baptized You."

Jesus nods, and His eyes fill with tears. "He and I were remarkably close...like you and Joseph are. The two of you remind Me of us." Joseph and I look at each other and smile.

Mary gently pats Jesus' hand. "I stayed with Elisabeth and her husband Zechariah for three months and then returned home. When Joseph found out I was pregnant, he did not believe my story, but he did not want me to be disgraced either. As he was trying to decide how to take care of things quietly, one night, an angel appeared to him in a dream saying to not worry about marrying me—the baby inside me was conceived by the Holy Ghost, not by another man. I would have a son to be named Jesus, and He will save His people from their sins. Being the faithful, just, and noble man that he was, Joseph and I were soon married."

"Before Jesus was born, Caesar Augustus sent out a decree for all the world to be taxed and counted. Since Joseph was from the house and lineage of David, we were required to go to the city of Bethlehem. The week-long journey from Nazareth to Bethlehem was not a pleasant one for me. We took the longer route avoiding Samaria and a smoother terrain, but I was in the final days of my pregnancy which made travel of any kind difficult. And when we finally arrived in Bethlehem, there was no room at the inn, and we had to stay in a nearby stable." She takes hold of Jesus' hand and smiles proudly. "But that is where my Jesus was delivered."

Jesus' face reddens, and He looks at the ground---this is the first time I have seen Jesus blush or look embarrassed. We all laugh.

"I knew Jesus was going to be special, but I did not realize it would begin as soon as it did. The night of His birth was a clear star-lit night—in fact, there was a very bright star directly overhead of the stable every night while we were in Bethlehem. A group of shepherds approached us and said a multitude of angels appeared to them and told them a Savior, Christ the Lord, was born in the city of David and could be found wrapped in swaddling clothes lying in a manger. They immediately came to see Him and apparently told others. People were coming from everywhere to see Jesus while we were in Bethlehem—even some wise men from the East had seen the star and came to worship Him. The magi brought Him gifts of gold, frankincense, and myrrh."

"While in Bethlehem, Joseph had another dream. And this time, the angel told him to take Jesus and me and flee to Egypt. King Herod was seeking to destroy Jesus because he heard the King of the Jews was born in Bethlehem. Joseph woke me, and we immediately left Bethlehem in the middle of the night. We later heard Herod had all the children in Bethlehem killed that were two years old and younger." She stares into space and shakes her head. "He was such an evil man. We lived in Egypt until Herod died, and an angel appeared to Joseph and said it was safe to return to Israel. Because Herod's son was now king and we were afraid to return to Bethlehem, we went to Nazareth instead. Both my parents had died by the time we returned, but I still had family there."

"Jesus has always been the perfect son, both as a child and as an adult." Jesus blushes again. "He always obeyed and honored God's law was always respectful and submissive to Joseph and me. I am sure His brothers and sisters thought we let Him get away with things since we never had to punish Him, but He never got into any trouble. He never fought with any of them like siblings do and was always watching over them and protecting them. There is only one time I can recollect He caused us any concern—He was not where He was supposed to be."

Peter laughs and pokes at Jesus. "Now we are going to hear some dirt about You."

Jesus laughs. "You are going to be extremely disappointed, Peter. Please continue, Mother."

"When Jesus was twelve, we went to Jerusalem for Passover like we did every year. The day after we left Jerusalem, we thought Jesus was with Elisabeth, Zechariah, and John—John the Baptist—until John came looking for Him."

Peter wags his finger at Jesus. "Uh-oh. I bet You got in trouble."

"We could not find him anywhere, so Joseph and I returned to Jerusalem. It took us three days to discover where He was. We found Him in the Temple court, sitting in the middle of all the rabbis, not only listening to them but questioning what they said. Like everyone around Him, we were amazed and shocked at His insight and His responses."

"When I told Him his father and I had been worried sick looking for Him and asked Him why He had done such a thing. I did not understand the meaning of His response at the time. But I do now, and I think all of you will too. I still remember His exact response as if it were yesterday."

Mary pauses and watches an ash flicker into the air and vanish. I asked the question I am sure everyone wanted to ask. "What was His answer?"

She looks at me and stands. "Why did you have to look for Me? Didn't you know I had to be concerning myself with my Father's affairs?" Mary yawns. "It's getting late, and I must get some rest now. Good night, fellows." She kisses Jesus on the top of His head and walks away.

# A WARM WELCOME

I lay on the ground looking at the twinkling stars on this clear spring night, wondering what we may encounter upon our arrival in Jerusalem. Everyone is either asleep or lost in their own thoughts. It is quiet except for the crackling fire warming us on a chilly night for this time of year.

Jesus' whereabouts are to be reported to the Jewish leaders, so how is He going to mingle with the huge crowds that gather for Passover without being captured? With the throng who are now here to see a living Lazarus, they must know He is already in the area. They probably already know exactly where He is. There will be many believers in Jerusalem, but there will also be many haters. Since He has predicted His death, maybe He will not be safe. Will any of us be? And now the life of Lazarus is at risk just because Jesus raised him from the dead? Are they going to kill everyone that Jesus has healed? I look around as someone pokes at the dying embers and stands warming themself. Their back is to me, so I cannot make out who it is. With the new warmth from the fire, I roll over and soon fall into a sound sleep.

Shortly after sunrise, we gather our belongings to complete the journey to Jerusalem for Passover. As we descend the Mount of Olives toward Bethphage, Jesus approaches Joseph and me. "Go into the village, and as you enter the gate, you will find a donkey tied to a tree that has never been ridden. Loose him and bring him to Me. If anyone asks why you are taking it, tell them the Lord needs him."

Judas Iscariot overhears Him. "Master, You should be riding on a horse—a stallion. Not a donkey. You need to enter Jerusalem with power and royalty. Show the Romans who is king."

Jesus shakes His head. "You still do not understand, do you, Judas? I am fulfilling the prophecy of Zechariah. I am here to bring peace to the children of Israel and the world. Not war."

With a grunt, Judas clenches his jaw, stiffens his body, turns, and walks away without saying a word. It is obvious, he does not agree with Jesus.

Jesus turns his attention back to Joseph and me. "Now go and fetch the donkey."

Joseph and I obey and run ahead of the group and enter the walled village of Bethphage. We spot the colt tied to a tree near the gate just as Jesus said we would. Nearby stands a group of men watching us as we cautiously approach the animal and begin untying it. The men briskly come to us, and one of them gruffly asks, "Why are you taking my colt?"

I answer as Jesus instructed. "The Lord needs him."

The man's demeanor changes immediately, and he smiles. "Please take him if the Lord needs him."

We thank the man and lead the colt to Jesus. The apostles cast their outer garments on the animal, and Jesus sits atop. Why is He riding a donkey into Jerusalem instead of walking as usual? This is only going to draw more attention to Himself. Is He trying to get arrested?

As we descend the hill into the Kidron Valley, the hillside is dotted with tents where people have already claimed their spots for the Passover festivities. As we draw near and they see it is Jesus on the donkey, they begin throwing their cloaks in front of Him. "Hosanna to the Son of David!" is shouted by many. Others cut branches from the trees and strew them in the way as if creating a royal path for Him. With John and Peter leading the donkey through the multitude and the remainder of the apostles closely at Jesus' side for protection, the people lining the road join the procession as we pass by them.

The chants of "Blessed is the King that comes in the name of the Lord!" grow even louder as we begin the ascent up the hill to the Temple Mount. People are crowding the path to catch a glimpse of Jesus, some pushing to get a better view. Garments and palm fronds continue to be thrown in front of Him. Those in the back of the crowd wave palm branches. Small children are on their fathers' shoulders, clapping with excitement while others jump up and down, waving as we move past. What a welcome—this is a sight to behold. The shouts greet us as we enter the eastern gate into the city. "Hosanna to the Son of David! Hosanna in the highest!" Watching in disgust, Pharisees are visible in the crowd. Surely, they will not try to accost Jesus with all these people around.

I spot Mother and Father in the mass of people but lose sight of them when I turn to tell Joseph. At least I know they are here. I will find them later when things are calmer. Since our family normally makes the trek from Bethsaida each year and stays at the home of Elizabeth's brother and his wife, Joseph and I know where they will be.

Jesus dismounts the donkey and enters the Temple. Since it is the Day of the Lamb, the Temple is packed with people as they select their sacrificial lambs for the Passover meal. He looks about and does not seem happy with what He sees. He briskly walks away.

Since eventide is approaching, He and "The Twelve" return to Bethany. Joseph and I go as far as Bethphage with them and return the donkey to its owner. After telling Peter and Andrew we are going to visit our family, we return to Jerusalem. After the warm welcome Jesus received today, I am confident we are safe.

Joseph and I receive a warm welcome, too, when we get back to Jerusalem. The sun has set as we approach the home of Micah, Elizabeth's brother. But it is still light enough to see the family standing outside the house. Joseph and I run to them, dodging people in our way. I grab Mother and Abba around their necks and kiss each one on the cheek. It has been a long time since I have seen them.

Micah hugs me. "When we heard Jesus was entering the city and you were with Him, we hoped you would come and stay with us."

"Thank you, Micah. We would not want to miss the traditional Passover with you."

Nava, Micah's wife, goes into the house and comes out carrying a tray of figs and cheese. "We already ate, but I am sure you are hungry. Please eat."

Joseph and I do not have to be persuaded. We clean the tray and talk well into the night, recapping our ventures with Jesus.

Benjamin turns his entire body toward me. "Be honest with us, Matthias. We keep hearing rumors there are threats to Jesus' life. What do you know? How safe are you and Joseph?"

I clear my throat, knowing what I am about to say is not what they want to hear—especially Mother and Abba. My parents are staring intently at me, waiting to hear my response. "The threats are real. Jesus has predicted His death is going to happen while we are here in Jerusalem." Everyone gasps.

"Our safety is not guaranteed either." I look at my parents to see their reactions. Mother's hands quickly cover her mouth as she buries her face into Abba's shoulder. Abba's eyes widen in disbelief as he tugs at his beard.

"How can that happen with the way Jesus was welcomed into the city today?" Seba squeezes Joseph's shoulder.

"Jesus has many believers, but He has many enemies, too. Especially with those in power. Jesus' whereabouts are supposed to be reported to them, and I am afraid they are waiting for the right opportunity to seize Him. We have been told the Pharisees and chief priests called a meeting with the Sanhedrin, and they are already plotting to kill Him. They have had plenty of time to devise a plan. Some Pharisees and scribes are in almost every crowd wherever Jesus teaches."

"Do whatever you must to remain safe, boys. I commend you for following the Messiah but be safe." Benjamin stands and yawns. "I am calling it a night."

Hugs are exchanged as everyone makes their way inside. Abba, Seba, Joseph, and I climb the ladder to sleep on the roof. Abba puts his hand on my shoulder, "Good night, son. I am proud of you, but please be cautious and stay safe. Your mother and I do not want to see anything bad happen to you."

"I will be careful, Abba."

# IN THE TEMPLE

The city is even more crowded today than yesterday. Many of the pilgrims have arrived early in order to purchase a sacrificial lamb or to procure a place to celebrate the Passover meal. Others are here to have the necessary rites of purification performed. Many have come early to gather with family and friends they may see only at Passover each year.

The streets will only get more crowded as the week continues. And with the increased number of pilgrims, the number of Roman guards will become more prominent and defensive against possible insurrection by the zealots. Rumors are already circulating through Jerusalem that there has already been one uprising, and a zealot has been imprisoned for killing a Roman guard. The guards will be eager to exert their power and revenge upon the Jews.

Joseph and I stroll to the Temple, and our timing is perfect. Jesus and "The Twelve" are approaching from the opposite direction. When we meet, Jesus does not acknowledge us—His eyes are fixed on the Temple entrance. We follow them into the Court of the Gentiles, the outer court of the Temple adorned with its colonnades where non-Jews from around the civilized world can come and worship God. Instead of finding Gentiles worshipping, we find the court crammed with tables of money changers and stalls of sacrificial animals. People are lined up at the tables, exchanging their local currency for the inflated Temple coins. Others are lined up at the stalls paying exorbitant prices for the sacrificial sheep or doves needed for the Passover rituals.

I have never seen Jesus get mad...until now. His face is beet red and wet with sweat. His jaws are tightly clenched, and His eyes are glassy. His hands are balled into fists. His nostrils flare with each quick step He takes to the first moneychanger's table. He grabs it at the corner and flips it into the air. Money flies everywhere. The moneychanger and those around his table grapple for the scattered coins. People scatter to make room as Jesus quickly moves down the row of tables, throwing each one as He passes. "Get out!" He knocks over the seats of those selling doves and opens the gates holding the sheep, allowing them to run amuck. "Get out! My house shall be called the house of prayer, but you have made it a den of thieves."

Pandemonium erupts. Afraid of what Jesus might do next, some of the merchants and moneychangers back away with their money boxes while the moneychangers fight with the patrons for the loose coins strewn on the Temple's floor. Some people rush for the exits, while others stand staring in shock. The sheep merchants run through the crowds trying to gather their flocks back into the open stalls. Those bird cages that are still intact are being grabbed by the vendors, or fights ensue as some in the crowd try to steal them. The freed birds are flying around the open area, trying to find their way out. "Get out! Get out!"

I stand frozen, not knowing what to do except watch as eventually, almost everyone exits the Temple. Luckily, there are no authorities nearby because He would surely be arrested for destroying the Temple's profitable business. Where are they? This would be the perfect opportunity for them to arrest Jesus.

A Greek family who is inside the Temple to worship approaches the Apostle Phillip and asks if they can see Jesus. Phillip tells Andrew, and they both go tell Jesus. I guess the family was too afraid to approach Jesus directly, especially after that tirade.

Although His face is still flushed, He has a calmer demeanor as He turns to face the Greek family. But He has an odd response, "The hour is come that the Son of man should be glorified. Unless a grain of wheat falls into the earth and dies, it remains alone. But if it dies, it bears much fruit." The Greeks look as confused as I feel. Is Jesus saying He must die to be glorified? And what does "glorified" mean?

Jesus tells them if anyone follows Him, one will be honored by the Father. "My soul is troubled. Should I ask the Father to save Me from this hour? This is why I came. Father, glorify thy name."

As people begin reentering the Temple, a thunderous voice from above the open area echoes through the courtyard for all to hear. "I have both glorified it and will glorify it again." I recognize the voice. Some are afraid and run back through the exits onto the streets. Many are asking where the voice came from or searching for who was speaking. The Greek family and a few others drop to their knees, knowing it was the voice of God.

Jesus explains the voice everyone heard. "This voice did not come because of Me, but for your sakes. Now is the judgment of this world. Now shall Satan, the prince of this world, be cast out. If the Son of Man be lifted from the earth, I will draw all men unto Me."

Someone in the crowd says that the Law teaches Christ will abide forever. "So, who is this Son of Man?"

His response is remarkably similar to what He told my parents when He first met them, "Only for a little while is the Light with you. Walk in the Light. Believe in the Light. Be children of the Light."

Jesus disappears into the crowd while they argue among themselves about who He is and what their messiah will accomplish. Some are expressing their belief in Jesus as their Messiah, while many say otherwise.

"The Romans will no longer be in power. This Man will save us."

"He is not the messiah. Our messiah would not disrespect the activities in the Temple like he did."

"He is here to establish an earthly kingdom that will never end. He is our Messiah."

"He's a blasphemer. He should be stoned."

Contrary to the crowd yesterday welcoming Him into Jerusalem, are the people turning against Him already? I am not feeling too confident about our safety anymore.

The next morning, the chief priests, scribes, and the elders confront Jesus as He walks into the Temple to teach. Knowing none of them taught Jesus in their schools or have authorized Him to teach in the Temple, they ask by what authority He is doing these things. They look confident they have trapped Him in front of the gathering crowd and repeat the question. "None of us taught you or gave you authority to teach in the Temple. Who gave You this authority?"

Jesus answers them with a question, "I will tell you by what authority I do these things if you can answer My question. The baptism of John—was it from heaven or from men? Answer me."

They are not so sure of themselves now. They huddle together close enough to where I can hear them whispering among themselves. "If we say from heaven, He will ask why we did not believe Him. How would we answer that question? And if we say from men, many in this crowd who believe John was a prophet will turn on us. They may even try to stone us." With heads down and not looking at anyone, especially Jesus, they sheepishly reply they do not know.

Some of the crowd hides giggles at their response, and especially when Jesus tells them since they could not answer His question, He was not going to answer them. Jesus sits and begins telling stories directed to the Jewish leaders—their self-righteous attitude will prevent them from entering the kingdom of God.

As a few of them turn and walk away, I overhear one of the scribes threatening to have Jesus arrested. One of his colleagues tells him to be patient. "Now is not the time. I do not know how the crowd will react—the majority of them are still believing He is their messiah today. We need to wait for a better opportunity to take Him."

Peter gives me a quick nod of acknowledgment when I glance at him to see if he heard the scribes. Why do they keep trying to trick Jesus? It is only making them look foolish in front of those they are supposed to teach about the Messiah. But they do not let it stop them.

"Teacher, we know You are true and teach the way of God." With a comment like this coming from a Pharisee, it is obvious they are up to something. "Is it lawful to pay taxes to Caesar?"

Jesus is not fooled and is obviously displeased. He crosses His arms and glares at them. "Why do you test Me, you hypocrites? Show me the tax money."

One of the Pharisees reaches into his pouch and pulls out a denarius, the standard silver coin for paying Roman taxes.

"Whose image is on the coin?"

They do not need to look at the coin to know the answer to this question, so they reply in unison, "Caesar."

"Render therefore to Caesar the things that are Caesar's and to God the things that are God's."

Stumped again, the Pharisees look frustrated and walk away. Jesus continues, "Woe to you, scribes and Pharisees. You tell the people to observe and do according to your works but do not these works yourselves. All your works are for the vain glory and to be seen by man. You make your phylacteries broad and enlarge the borders of your garments for attention. You sit in the most prominent seats. You will receive the greatest condemnation."

One of the Pharisees looks back red-faced but does not respond. What will they do next?

The Sadducees then present a ridiculous scenario, especially since they do not believe in the resurrection of the body after death. But they present it anyway. "According to the Law of Moses, the Law of the Goel decrees if a man dies childless, then the brother of that man is to marry and provide for the widow and give her children. After the death of her husband, each of his six brothers marries this widow and dies without fathering a child. Finally, the woman dies. In the resurrection, to whom is she married?"

I do not know if anyone else notices, but Jesus has a slight smirk on His face when He answers. He would probably laugh at them if He did not feel so sorry for their ignorance. "If you knew the Scriptures or power of God, you would already know the answer to that question. In the resurrection, they neither marry nor are given in marriage. They are equal to the angels and are sons of God, being sons of the resurrection. God is not the God of the dead, but of the living."

The Sadducees back away when one of the scribes nods his head in agreement. "Teacher, You have spoken well." What an unexpected change—a scribe agreeing with Jesus.

# THE SEDER

Joseph and I join Jesus, "The Twelve," and a few other disciples on the Mount of Olives. We sit at Jesus' feet as tears run down His cheeks. He scans the panoramic view of Jerusalem and warns us of its upcoming total destruction by Gentile armies. "Do not hesitate when you see them coming. Flee the city at once—there will be no time for delay." He wipes away more tears at the thought. I wish He would tell us when it is going to occur, but He does not, and no one asks.

Jesus tells us of things to look for at the end of time—false christs, wars, famines, earthquakes. "The sun will not shine. The moon will not give light. The stars of heaven will fall from the sky. After that tribulation, the Son of Man will come in the clouds with great power and glory. He will send His angels and gather together His elect."

His final words chill me to the bones. "In two days is the feast of the Passover, and the Son of Man will be betrayed and will be crucified."

With my arms crossed over my knees, I rest my face on them, trying to choke back the tears. They come anyway. Without looking up, I know whose hand is on my shoulder. "It is the Father's plan, Matthias." Jesus' calm voice and soothing touch are consoling, but I cannot imagine Jesus—my Messiah hanging on a Roman cross.

Jesus and his apostles head toward Bethany while Joseph and I descend the Mount to return to the home of Micah and Nava. The city of Jerusalem really is beautiful from up here. It is hard to imagine it crumbled in ruins.

"I have never heard Jesus talk with that tone before. I hate to say this, but He sounded like the voice of doom. He really does believe He is going to be killed."

Joseph stops, turns, and waits for me to take the needed steps, so we are side-by-side. "I hope His predictions are wrong this time. They do sound dismal—for Him and possibly us."

It is the morning of the Day of Unleavened Bread, and many of the pilgrims are bustling around Jerusalem, making last-minute preparations for the Passover meal. However, there are not as many people on the streets as in the last few days. I guess they are in their homes preparing for their families and guests to gather for the Feast.

While all the chametz, the leavening or grain that ferments causing bread to rise, is eradicated from the house by Martha, Nava, Rachel, and Mother, the males are asked to go outside and tend to the fire while it is burned. The women bring out the last of any leavening found in the house and toss it in the fire. They need to make the matzah now.

I see Peter and John exit a house two doors down the street. Since I did not see them yesterday, I run to greet them. "What are you two doing here? I thought you would be in Bethany."

Peter hugs me. "Jesus sent us to secure an upper room and prepare for the Passover. He told us we would see a man carrying a jar of water, and we were to follow him. Since that is a woman's job, Joab was easy to find. We followed him to this house and told him The Teacher needed a place to celebrate the Passover. It helped he is a believer Jesus is our Messiah, and he took us to a large room upstairs. He said we could use it for as long as we needed, so we are making final preparations for the meal now. All we have left to do is purchase the lamb and have it slain by the priest—and of course, roast it."

I point to the home of Micah and Nava. "Hopefully, I will see you later since you will be so close. This is where Joseph and I are staying."

"Maybe we will see you after the meal. But we need to hurry to get everything done." Peter and John wave goodbye as they rush down the street toward the Temple.

Between the burning leavening, matza being baked, and lambs roasting over the open fires throughout the city, my mouth waters in anticipation of the meal.

When the sun sets, it is time for the Passover meal to begin. We all sit on pillows placed around the low table so we can recline during the meal to remind us of our freedom from Egyptian slavery. Wine is poured into kiddush goblets. Three matzot are placed on a plate and covered with a cloth reminding us of the hurried departure from Egyptian captivity. On each of our plates is matzah, maror, charoset, karpas, and beitzah. Bowls of saltwater are conveniently located for dipping the karpas. Pitchers of water, bowls, and towels for handwashing are also on the table.

Special attention is given to the placement of each of the symbolic foods on the plate. Maror, the bitter horseradish root reminding us of our ancestors' suffrage in slavery, is placed in the center of each plate. It is surrounded by beitzah, pesach, charoset, and karpas. Karpas, parsley with its green leaves, represents spring and, when dipped in saltwater, signifies the Israelites' tears. Pesach is the roasted bone symbolizing the first-born lamb sacrificed as the Passover offering. Charoset is the tastiest of anything on the seder plate. It is a mixture of fruits, nuts, and wine prompting us to remember the mortar used by the Israelite slaves in building the Egyptian palaces and pyramids. Beitzah, the roasted egg, is also a sign of spring.

Since Micah is the host of this meal, he welcomes us to the table by reciting a Hebrew blessing. Following the traditional order of the seder meal, he pours each of us a cup of wine and recites the blessing. "Our people suffered under the yoke of slavery, and Yahweh promised our deliverance. We raise the first cup and repeat God's promise to our ancestors and to us."

Although the Passover meal is a holy event, it is also a time for fellowship and fun for family and friends. I look at Joseph as he drains his cup of wine, and he is already resting on his elbow on the pillow. I point and laugh. "You don't look like you are going to make it through the meal, Joseph."

"I drank that cup a little too fast."

The rest of the family joins in the kidding until we all finish our wine. A bowl of water and a towel are passed around for us to wash our hands. Micah then recites the blessing over the green vegetable, and we dip our parsley into the saltwater. It is difficult to swallow the bitter and salty greens after just having the sweet wine.

Lifting the plate with the three matzot, Micah breaks the middle one into two pieces. He wraps the larger piece in a napkin as the Israelites wrapped their kneading bowls in their cloaks in preparation to leave Egypt. It is normally then hidden for children to find at the end of the meal, but since there are none in this household, that part is skipped. That was always my favorite part of the Seder meal when I was a child, and I was looking forward to my son experiencing it. But he never will.

The Exodus story is told, and Micah reads the scripture pertaining to each of the ten plagues inflicted upon the Egyptians prior to the Exodus. He tells how Yahweh used each plague to execute His judgment and display His power over the various gods of Egypt, starting with the god of the Nile and ending with Pharaoh himself. After each plague is read and discussed, we each dip our finger into our cup and remove a drop of wine. After singing a song of praise, the Hallel, we have the second cup of wine and wash our hands again. The three matzot are uncovered and raised, the blessing is recited, and pieces of the top and middle matzot are distributed. We taste the matzah, and conversation resumes. We all stand and stretch.

The bitter herbs are blessed, and the maror is dipped in the charoset and placed between two pieces of matzah, forming the Hillel. Although it is not much, the Hillel and egg are welcomed to my empty and growling stomach. Especially after two cups of wine.

The Seder meal concludes with the eating of the half piece of the middle matzot, which is divided among each of us so we can have one last taste of matzah. Micah leads the blessing after the meal while we respond. Then we have the third cup of wine. We all raise our cups and again repeat God's promise to our ancestors and to us

Since we have now had quite a bit of wine and none of us can carry a tune, we all laugh at and make fun of each other as we sing the songs of praise. As if needed, we follow tradition and raise the fourth cup of wine and repeat God's promise before concluding the Seder meal with singing the Hillel.

Everyone is tired from the day's events and ready to sleep. Since Joseph and I are planning to sleep on the roof, we go outside and climb the ladder. I get to the top rung and hear footsteps on the hard street below. I stand up, peer over the side of the roof, and see Peter and John walking beside Jesus, followed closely by the other apostles. Andrew is lagging behind, slowly shuffling along.

I scurry down the ladder and run to where they are. Since they are already past the entrance to the house of Micah and Nava, I run to Andrew. "Where are all of you going this late?"

"To the Garden of Gethsemane to pray. Come and join us."

I turn to Joseph. "Let's go."

I run back to the house, stick my head in the door, and tell Abba where Joseph and I are going. "We will be back soon."

Andrew is walking slowly with his head down, watching each step he takes, falling farther and farther behind Jesus and the apostles. Joseph and I catch up with him easily. He looks up at me but quickly drops his gaze to the ground. "What's wrong, Andrew? What has happened?"

"It is not what has happened. It is what is about to happen."

"What do you mean?"

"Jesus told us at the meal one of the apostles will betray Him. He said it would be the one He gave the bread to after He had dipped it."

He looks up. "It was Judas Iscariot. Judas immediately left the room after that. We do not know where he went or why he left. Joab said he ran out of the house and down the street out of sight."

Tears well up in my eyes. "Oh, no. This cannot be happening. What can we do?"

"There is more. Jesus told us we would all desert Him—we would all leave Him to suffer alone. I want to prove Him wrong, but He hasn't been wrong yet." Tears are rolling down Andrew's cheeks. He stops walking, squats, and buries his head in his hands. "I have never been afraid of conflict before, but I am scared of what might happen to all of us now. I have been lingering behind this whole time because a part of me wants to turn and run away. But where would I go? I would not be able to live with myself if I deserted Jesus and the other apostles."

I do not know if I can say anything that will benefit Andrew, so I remain silent. So does Joseph. We each put a hand on Andrew's shoulders and let him cry. I have been so concerned about Andrew; I have not thought about what I will do...until now while it is quiet.

Andrew regains his composure, stands, and says we need to hurry and catch up to the rest of the group. Now I feel like running away from them, not toward them. I am scared, too.

# IN THE GARDEN

We exit the eastern gate and head north on the road that runs alongside the Kidron Valley. Crossing the brook at the base of the Mount of Olives, we enter a grove of gnarled olive trees, the Garden of Gethsemane. A cool breeze blows through the trees. Andrew whispers. "Jesus has come here to pray every night this week."

When we pass the olive press, Jesus stops and tells Peter, James, and John to join Him. He wants the remainder of us to stay here and "watch and pray." The moonlight is bright enough to where I can see Him take Peter, James, and John a bit farther into the garden. I can hear them talking but am too far away to understand what is being said. Peter, James, and John sit on the ground, and Jesus goes about a stone's throw further, kneels, and bows His head.

The remaining apostles make themselves comfortable leaning against trees or laying on the ground. A few are already dozing off, including Joseph. Someone is snoring. Within a few minutes, I am the only one of them still awake—I am not sure what we are supposed to be watching for, but whatever it is will not be seen by this group.

I am curious, so I sneak away from the sleeping group and find a tree I can hide behind where I can watch and hear Jesus but not be seen by Peter, James, and John. They are not seeing anything—they are asleep, too.

Jesus raises His hands to the sky. His voice is shaky when He cries out. "Oh, My Father, if it is possible, let this cup pass from Me. Nevertheless, not as I will, but as You will."

He puts His head down into His hands, and His shoulders shake. I want to go hug Him and console Him, but He wipes His eyes and stands. He approaches Peter, James, and John and nudges Peter with His foot. Peter looks up groggily from his slumber. "What...could you not watch with Me one hour? Watch and pray lest you enter into temptation. The spirit is willing, but the flesh is weak."

Jesus returns to where He was praying. Peter has already rolled over and fallen back asleep. Jesus looks back at the sleeping apostles, slowly shakes His head, falls prostrate on the ground, and sobs. "Abba, Father. All things are possible with You. If it is Your will, please take this cup away from Me."

He rises and goes to where Peter, James, and John are sleeping. Obviously disappointed when He sees the three apostles asleep, Jesus briefly covers His face with His hands and quietly weeps. He stares at them for a little while but does not wake them this time.

When Jesus walks back to His prayer spot, He kneels, putting His head to the ground. "Father, if it is Your will, take this cup away from Me. Not My will, but Your will be done."

A cloud covers the moon, and it is so dark I can barely make out the silhouette of Jesus. I muffle a gasp as a spirit or an angel descends from the cloud and kneels next to Jesus, placing its hand upon Jesus' back. Jesus is in such agony when He looks up; the sweat falling from His face is like drops of blood. The angel embraces Jesus holding Him tightly, then fades into the darkness.

The moon illuminates the area, and I can now clearly see Jesus stand and wipe His face on the sleeve of His robe. He walks slowly with a panged look on His face toward Peter, James, and John. He wakes the sleeping trio this time. "Are you still sleeping? Behold, the hour is at hand, and the Son of Man is being betrayed into the hands of sinners. Rise, let us be going."

He points toward a group of torches entering the Garden. "See. My betrayer is at hand."

Peter, James, and John leap to their feet. Peter puts his hand on the handle of his sword but leaves it in place. In the few seconds it takes to rejoin the other apostles and Joseph, the group of captors is upon us. To my amazement, Judas Iscariot is leading some of the chief priests, elders, and a detachment of troops and Temple guards with drawn swords. He approaches Jesus and kisses Him. "Rabbi."

Taking hold of Judas' shoulders, Jesus stares into his eyes. Tears roll down Jesus' cheeks. "Are you betraying the Son of Man with a kiss?"

Judas pulls away and runs into the crowd. Jesus steps forward and looks at the group. "Who are you seeking?"

"Jesus of Nazareth."

"I am."

They shrink back, and some fall to the ground. With most being Jews, I feel certain they know the term "I am" refers to God. I do not know if they backed up and fell out of fear, reverence, or both.

The scenario repeats itself, except this time, they seize Jesus and bind His hands. Peter pulls out his sword and swings it at one of the captor's heads. The captor is quick and dodges the blow. Instead of losing his head, the guard only loses an ear. He screams in pain and falls to the ground grabbing his head where his ear once was. The Temple guards quickly advance toward us, and some of the apostles run deeper into the garden. Simon, the zealot, draws his sword and gets in a defensive stance.

"Stop!" Jesus tells Peter to put away his sword. "He who lives by the sword will die by the sword." Peter looks at Jesus and opens his mouth to argue, but he remains quiet. He is slow to obey and puts his sword back in the sheath. Simon, the zealot, does the same.

Even though His hands are bound, Jesus is still in control of the situation. The guards allow Him to approach the man wriggling on the ground in pain. Jesus touches his ear, the bleeding stops, and his wound is healed. Still kneeling, the man looks up at Jesus and thanks Him, then is lost in the hostile group shackling Jesus. A miracle was performed on one of their own, but they are not fazed by it.

Someone shouts, "Shall we arrest the others?"

Without waiting to hear an answer, the remaining apostles, Joseph, and I run. When I feel I am a safe distance away, I duck behind a bush and look back to see if we are being chased. Jesus is being pulled by the chain attached to the iron collar like an animal. He stumbles, falls, and is immediately backhanded by one of His captors. The guard snatches Him by the hair and shoves Him forward.

I cannot watch anymore—my eyes are too clouded with tears. We deserted our Messiah—I deserted my Messiah.

Oh, God! Jesus' prediction is coming true.

I flinch when a hand touches my shoulder and jerk my head around to see who it is. Whew. It is Peter. He kneels beside me, puts his arm around me, and whispers in my ear, "Yes, His prediction is coming true."

I did not realize I had said my thoughts out loud. We sit quietly and watch until the blaze of the torches goes out of sight. His compassionate embrace is comforting, but I still feel helpless. "What do we do now, Peter?"

We hear footsteps approaching from behind. Peter quickly draws his sword as he springs to his feet.

"There is no need for that, Peter. It is just us." Andrew runs and hugs Peter. "I am glad you are safe." Peter does not say anything. He sobs on his brother's shoulder while Joseph, John, and I watch the brothers.

Although we all are glad to see each other is safe, we are all very glum and saddened by what just happened. Not only is our Messiah in the hands of His enemies, but we stand here unscathed after deserting Him. I am ashamed of my cowardice as I feel they are.

John breaks the silence. "We looked around but have not seen any of the other apostles. I do not know where they went. Let us go see where they take Jesus. Maybe there is something we can do."

We trot through the trees until we get to a clearing and catch a glimpse of the angry mob as they pull Jesus through the east gate to Jerusalem. Although there seems to be no interest in us by the time we enter the gate, we do not take any chances. Trying to not look suspicious, we mingle with the few people that are milling around at this time of night. There are not many in the streets tonight, especially since most were celebrating the Passover earlier in the evening.

# THE JEWISH TRIAL

Although Annas is not the high priest, the mob leads Jesus to his palatial palace. He is the head of the most prominent high-priestly family and wields a lot of power in Jerusalem. Not only is he the leader of the Sanhedrin, the pious seventy-one-member Jewish ruling council over the Temple and religious courts, but He and his family collaborated with the Romans and supplied most of the high priests appointed by Roman governors, including several of his sons and his son-in-law Caiphas. For Annas to be bothered at this time of night, he must be expecting Jesus to be brought to him and probably the one who got this group together so quickly.

We follow them as far as we can. I am not sure how John knows the high priest, but he tells us to wait here outside the iron gate to see if he can get permission for us to enter the courtyard. He comes back and talks to one of the servant girls, then walks to where we are standing. "Only one of you can enter. Peter, come in with me. The rest of you are going to have to stay out here, and one of us will let you know what is happening as soon as we can."

As they enter the courtyard, the servant girl stops Peter. "Haven't I seen you with this Man being questioned? Aren't you one of His disciples?"

I am surprised at Peter's emphatic response to her question. "I am not." John does a double-take and grabs Peter's arm. He whispers something to him and then enters the private residence leaving Peter in the courtyard.

I turn toward Andrew and Joseph and whisper. "Why did he just deny knowing Jesus?"

Andrew is shaking his head and mumbling. "No, Peter. Don't do it."

"Do what, Andrew?"

Andrew does not respond to my question. Joseph shrugs his

shoulders and offers an excuse. "He probably feels he will be taken prisoner, too."

As we peer through the gate, Peter walks to the fire pit where some of the guards are warming themselves. I do not understand what is being said by Peter and the group of men standing around the fire, but suddenly Peter loudly announces that he is not one of the disciples and hurriedly walks toward us.

Andrew covers his mouth and stares at Peter. Tears fill Andrew's eyes. "No, Peter. Please don't do it."

Peter stops and looks as Jesus is shoved out the palace door and loses his footing on the steps. The guards jerk Jesus up to His feet and lead Him across the courtyard. His eye and jaw are swollen—He looks like He has been in a fight. There is blood around His neck and wrists from where the fetters have cut into His skin. The manacles around His ankles cause Him to stumble and fall, and He grunts as one of the guards kicks Him in the ribs. "Get up, your majesty." The guards jerk on the chains attached to the iron collar and laugh when He tumbles to the ground again.

One of the guards confronts Peter as he points to Jesus, "You chopped off the ear of my cousin tonight. You were with Him in the garden."

Peter begins to curse loudly and swear. "I do not know this man you are talking about."

The cock crows twice while Jesus is still on His hands and knees. He and Peter exchange glances. Peter bursts into tears and runs out the gate past us. Andrew chases him but soon returns alone. "He was too fast—I do not know where he went, but another one of Jesus' predictions just came true."

I tilt my head and give Andrew a blank look. "Jesus told Peter he would deny Him three times before the cock crows twice. Of course, Peter argued it would never happen. And I did not believe it would either, but we all have seen it. He must feel awful, especially since

Jesus was looking directly at him." Andrew brushes his tears away with the back of his hand.

John walks toward us but stands just inside the gate close to us so as not to draw attention. He speaks in a low voice, "Annas is sending Jesus to Caiphas and the Sanhedrin."

As the sun peaks over the top of the eastern walls on this brisk spring morning and the torches are extinguished, several of the Sanhedrin stand outside the home of Caiphas, the high priest, and watch Jesus being led inside. I do not know who John knows, but he follows the group entering the home and disappears behind the massive closed doors.

When he eventually comes out, he walks to us, shaking his head. His face is pale. "The Sanhedrin called several witnesses—mostly false witnesses. Two of them claimed to hear Jesus say He could destroy the Temple and rebuild it in three days. As you know, destroying the Temple would be an offense worthy of death, but Caiphas asked Jesus if He was the Messiah. When Jesus responded, 'I am,' and they would see Him at the right hand of God, Caiphas charged Him with blasphemy." He leans forward, resting his hands on his knees. "They sentenced Him to death. When Caiphas tore his garment, so did many of the other elders...and then pandemonium broke out. They began spitting in Jesus' face and beat Him. They even blindfolded Jesus and would hit Him and then ask Him who it was that struck Him. I had to get out of there. I could not watch anymore."

We all stare when John breaks down and is unable to speak. Andrew tugs at his beard. He pats John on the shoulder. "It's not over, right? Under Roman rule, the Sanhedrin can try civil and religious cases, but don't the Romans try criminal cases?"

"Yes, they are sending Him to Pontius Pilate for execution... whenever they finish doing whatever to Him."

Andrew tries to reassure us, "So, there is still hope."

We all stare as the massive doors open, and Jesus is pulled out. The captors wait until He is out the door to remove the blindfold. Jesus can barely blink His swollen eyes to adjust His vision to the morning sun. Blood is running from a busted lip. Spittle remains on His cheeks and beard from the taunting.

Caiphas follows them—his hands gripping his robe, making sure everyone sees it is ripped open to his waist, revealing a bare chest. He points to Jesus and announces the sentence of death due to blasphemy to those watching and smiles at the spectacle when most of the crowd cheer and join the parade led by the prisoner and the Sanhedrin to the palace of Pontius Pilate.

I stare for a second, then drop my gaze to the ground. This cannot be happening.

# THE ROMAN TRIAL

Jesus is mocked by the guards and Sanhedrin the entire way to the Praetorium or hall of judgment at the Antonia Fortress on the northwest corner of the Temple Mount. Not only does it function as the housing and headquarters of the Roman garrison who guard the Temple courts, but it also contains the palace of Pontius Pilate, the Roman governor of Judea.

Since entering the home of a Gentile causes a Jewish person to be ceremoniously unclean, the Sanhedrin call for Pilate to come outside. Hearing the commotion outside his palace, Pilate comes out to them and leans on the balcony tapping his fingers on the rail. He is not happy with what he sees as the guards shove Jesus in front of him.

"What is this about? What is this Man accused of?"

"If He were not a criminal, we would not have delivered Him to you. He claims to be the Messiah, the king to rule over all people."

"Take Him and judge Him according to your law."

"We can't. It is not lawful for us to put any man to death."

"To death? What is this man charged with?"

"Blasphemy."

"And you want Him killed for that? Bring Him to me then."

The Sanhedrin remain outside as the guards shove Jesus through the palace doors. The crowd quickly grows larger and louder at the encouragement of the Sanhedrin while Pilate is questioning Jesus on the other side of the closed doors. Chants of "Crucify Him" spread through the mass.

Jesus is thrust through the palace doors, and pandemonium erupts when Pilate announces to the crowd that he finds no fault with Jesus.

"He stirs up the people beginning from Galilee to this place."

"If He is Galilean, then He is in Herod's jurisdiction. Take Him there."

The guards take their frustrations out on Jesus as we walk to the royal palace of Herod Antipas. They yank on the chains making Him stumble and fall to the amusement of many in the crowd. When He falls, they drag Him along until He gets on His feet. They push and shove through the crowd, which is growing larger as the sun rises higher in the sky. By the time we arrive, Jesus' palms and knees are bleeding.

It does not take long for Herod to decide. The guards mock and bow to Him as Jesus exits the palace wearing one of Herod's robes. "To Pilate, your majesty."

As the crowd grows larger, so does the vocal mob of Jesus haters. Where did they all come from? Although some in the crowd are followers of Jesus, out of fear, most remain quiet. Where are all of Jesus' followers?

Mary, the mother of Jesus, and Mary Magdalene join us en route to the Praetorium. When the mother of Jesus sees Him, she must lean on John for support and buries her face into his chest.

Pilate is not happy to see this group again. "I have already told you I find no fault in Him at all. What do you want?"

"Crucify the blasphemer."

"For what? I find no fault in Him."

The chants grow louder, and the crowd begins pushing toward the palace entrance. The Roman guards push back, but the angry mob keeps shoving their way forward.

Pilate leans against his throne and holds up his hand. "Silence!"

The crowd quietens. "You have a custom I should release unto you one at the Passover—the way your people were released from Egyptian captivity. Do you want me to release the King of the Jews, as you call Him?"

"He is not our king. Crucify Him!"

"No! Crucify this man."

Pilate turns to his guards and orders them to bring out a prisoner named Barrabas. He points to a big, burly man bound in chains, who is resisting being brought before the crowd by three Roman guards. Barabbas is known to have led a failed insurrection against the Roman government and is accused of murdering one soldier.

Pilate points to Jesus. "I ask you again. Do you want me to release this Man?

"Not this Man, but Barabbas!"

"Release Barabbas!"

"Crucify Jesus!"

"Away with this Man. Release Barabbas!

There are a few cries to release Jesus, but our cries are overwhelmed with the thunderous cries to release Barabbas. Pilate must think he can appease the crowd by having Jesus scourged in the common hall and sends Him away before passing sentence. Even he does not see justice in having Jesus crucified.

I can understand Mary, the mother of Jesus, wanting to stay close to her son, but cannot imagine her having to watch the torture He is about to experience. She, Mary Magdalene, and John follow Him. I have heard stories about the Roman scourges and do not ever want to witness one. The prisoner is stripped and strapped to a post. Two or more lictors trained in the art of inflicting pain take turns striking the victim with the flagrum made of leather braided with bits of stone, metal, and glass. The stone bruises the body while the metal and glass rip away chunks of flesh. The prisoner is beaten until he has just enough strength to carry his cross to the crucifixion site.

I see Abba, Seba, and Benjamin at the back of the crowd. Andrew, Joseph, and I make our way to them, and Abba grabs me around the neck, hugging me tightly. "We have been worried about all of you since you didn't return to Micah's house last night. We heard Jesus was arrested, but nothing about anyone else. What is happening?"

I know I probably look childish, but I do not care. I do not want to let go of Abba or leave his comforting embrace. I let Andrew summarize everything. As Andrew finishes talking, Pilate exits the palace and sits on the judgment seat. My legs buckle when the Roman soldiers bring Jesus out. Abba and Benjamin catch me before I fall.

Jesus' hair is matted with blood, where they forced a woven crown of thorns down to His brow. Blood is trickling down His face into His almost-closed swollen eyes and beard. Although a purple robe is draped over His naked body, it does not entirely hide the wounds inflicted by the brutal lashing from the lictors. Muscle and tendons are visible from the missing chunks of flesh. Blood trickles down His legs and puddles around His shackled feet. If it was not for the guard holding Him and the reed in His right hand, I think He would be too weak to stand.

Although I am sure he has seen plenty of prisoners tortured by the lictors, Pilate cannot even look at Jesus directly. He leans back on his throne, quickly shaking his head as if trying to forget what he just saw. He stands, clears his throat, and points to Jesus while looking at the Sanhedrin, "Behold the Man."

They immediately shout and are joined by the crazed throng, "Crucify Him! Crucify Him!"

Pilate raises his hands for everyone to be quiet. "I find no fault in Him."

"Our laws say He should die because He made Himself the Son of God. If you let this Man go, you are not a friend of Caesar. Whoever makes himself a king speaks against Caesar."

"Behold your King—King of the Jews."

"Away with Him. Crucify Him."

"Shall I crucify your King? What evil has He done?"

"We have no king but Caesar. Crucify Him!"

Pilate throws his hands up in defeat and shakes his head. He takes a pan of water and washes his hands so the multitude can see. "I am innocent of the blood of this just Man. See to it yourselves."

The Sanhedrin are ecstatic about winning this battle. "His blood is on us and our children." The crowd is in a frenzy—clapping, hollering, jumping up and down.

The purple robe is snatched from Jesus' shoulders, sending fresh droplets of blood into the crowd. The frenzied mass cheers louder. The guards throw His own robe over His shoulders, covering His raw, bloody chest and back. People are pushing and shoving to get the best view as the guards take Him to bear His cross.

Judas Iscariot runs to us breathless and grabs my shoulder. He cannot stand still and holds up a bag that jingles like it is filled with coins. He cannot seem to take his stare away from Jesus. "I've got to stop this. This was not supposed to happen. Where is Caiphas? I've got to stop this!"

"He was at the front of the crowd with the Sanhedrin earlier. I don't know if he is still...."

Judas sprints into the crowd, pushing people out of his way, screaming Caiphas' name but is drowned by the cheers for Jesus' crucifixion. Andrew follows him.

# THE ROAD TO GOLGOTHA

The Roman guards place the heavy crossbeam on the shredded shoulders of Jesus. Each arm is tied with a coarse rope to help balance the wooden beam, and Jesus is hoisted to His feet. Blood soaks through the shoulders of His robe as He staggers to get His balance. The beam presses against the crown of thorns gouging into His head, causing blood to trickle down His face. He blinks to try and clear His vision of the fresh blood in His eyes.

His knees tremble as He takes the first step. Snap goes the sound of a whip from one of the guards behind Him. "You need to move faster than that, your Highness." The guards laugh as another crack of the leather strap wraps around His body. He jerks in pain but remains upright and exits the Praetorium onto the crowded street where people are ecstatic, although a few cover their faces and back into the shadows to avoid the ghastly sight. Insults are shouted at Him by others. Some hock sputum into His face as He passes them, and the saliva mixed with blood runs into His eyes and beard. Others throw dirt in His face.

Joseph and I weave our way through the mass, leaving Abba, Seba, and Benjamin behind. The guards in front and to the side of Jesus push people out of the way who are crowding the street to see the gruesome parade and hurl more insults. Another lash of a whip encircles Jesus' body and brings Him to His knees. The weight of the crossbeam shifts and crushes His thorn-crowned head to the ground. Blood drips from the new deeper wounds.

Two guards come up on each side of Him, grab the beam, and jerk it up, so Jesus is standing. "Now walk!" From hitting the hard street, Jesus' jaw is busted open and oozing blood.

He totters to one side, then the other but regains His balance and exits the Garden Gate. The crowd continues to shout insults at Him and spit on Him as He passes. The guards do not slow down their verbal and physical abuse either. Another whiplash. "We don't have all day, King of the Jews. Move faster!"

People line the path outside the gate of the Holy City to witness Jesus' slow, arduous trek to Golgotha. Mary, the mother of Jesus, is on her knees in tears, while John and Mary Magdalene try to comfort her—it is for naught. Many of the Sanhedrin are here to witness Jesus' final steps to the crucifixion to ensure He is killed. Barely able to walk, Jesus continues to carry His cross toward His ultimate destination.

Jesus' legs tremble, and He crumples to the ground under the weight of the heavy piece of wood. The snap of the whip causes no reaction by Jesus. A guard grabs Jesus to make Him stand but turns to the centurion in charge. The guard shakes his head as he looks at his superior officer. "I do not think He is going to make it. Someone else needs to carry the crossbeam up the hill."

The officer points to a large, muscular dark-skinned man. "You. Help the King carry His cross."

At first, the man refuses and backs away. But two Roman guards seize him and force him to where Jesus is laying on the ground under the beam. Jesus' arms remain tied to the beam as two guards hoist Him to His feet. Fresh blood drips from the thorny crown as He tries to regain His balance. Jesus' legs will not support Him as He tries to stand. He falls to His knees. The man moves under the crossbeam to bear its weight, and Jesus leans upon the man for support. They slowly ascend the hill—Jesus can barely move His feet to walk. By the time they reach the summit, the man's arms and robe are splotched and smeared with Jesus' blood. As he is freed from his task, I hear Jesus hoarsely say thank you to him. The man turns and looks back at Jesus before running into the crowd.

The guards untie the ropes to the crossbeam and fasten the beam into a notch on a roughly hewn flat log. Jesus grimaces in pain as they jerk the robe, which has now stuck to His old wounds, causing them to reopen and bleed. The guards throw Him onto the rough log and pull Him across the splintered wood until they have Him in place. The thorny crown digs into Jesus' head. A guard pulls Jesus' hand into position on the crossbeam while others hold His body in place. Jesus is too weak to resist. Another one approaches with a mallet and large spike, places the point of the spike in the palm of Jesus' hand, and hammers the spike into the crosspiece. Bam! Bam! Bam! Jesus lurches in pain with each blow as blood spurts from the wound.

I break into a sweat, am nauseated, and run behind a bush to vomit. The centurion sees me and laughs. "What is the matter, boy? Down on your knees, throwing up. Is that any way to bow before your King?" Several of the guards point and laugh.

They repeat the process with the other hand. I cannot watch and cover my ears to try and drown the sound of the pounding hammer. I still hear the Bam... Bam... Bam. I swallow hard. I gag and vomit again. I watch them place a wooden pedestal at Jesus' feet and hammer it in place. I turn my head when they place His feet on the pedestal to drive a spike through them. Bam! Bam! Bam! A board saying "THIS IS THE KING OF THE JEWS" is nailed above His head, written in Greek, Latin, and Hebrew.

Four guards grab the crossbeam and lift it up. Another guides the cross to the edge of a deep hole. As they lift the cross into an upright position, the cross slides into the hole with an abrupt jolt that jars Jesus' body. He squints His eyes and grits His teeth in pain as His arms are pulled taut, and the nails in His hands support the weight of His body. Blood flows down His arms and streams down his sides, dripping onto the ground.

Upright beams of the crosses of former crucifixions are scattered atop the hillside. They provide a dismal background for the cruel sentencing of an innocent man.

# ON THE CROSS

With all my attention focused on the events surrounding Jesus, the hours have passed quickly, and it is already mid-morning. I imagine with the torture Jesus has been enduring, it must seem like an eternity for Him. I did not notice two other men being crucified until now. Although they were flogged, too, they did not receive the beating and abuse Jesus did. When their crosses are erected on each side of Jesus, their crosses are almost touching His. When the guards let the bloodthirsty crowd move closer, the chief priests begin mocking and taunting Jesus.

"He saved others, but He can't save Himself."

"You are going to destroy the Temple and rebuild it in three days. You cannot even save Yourself."

"Come down from the cross, Messiah, so we can see and believe."

"Come down from the cross if you are the Son of God."

"He trusts in God. Let God rescue Him now...if God wants Him."

Jesus presses His feet against the wooden platform and pushes His body up in an attempt to relieve the pressure on His hands and arms. He takes a deep breath and looks at the Roman guards...the crowd...and then the Jewish elders standing in front of Him. "Father, forgive them for they know not what they do."

"We know exactly what we are doing, blasphemer."

One of the criminals being crucified joins in the ridiculing. "Aren't you the Messiah? Save Yourself and us."

The other criminal rebukes him, "Do you not fear God since you are under the same sentence? We are going to die here, too. We are being justly punished. We are getting what our deeds deserve. But this Man has done nothing wrong. Jesus, remember me when You come into Your kingdom."

Jesus turns His head toward the man. "Truly I tell you, today you will be with Me in paradise."

A Sadducee joins in, "Paradise. Hah! There is no resurrection. Your eternity will all be spent in a cold grave."

It is difficult to look at Jesus' battered face. But even in its beaten, bruised, and swollen condition, He looks at them with mercy and mouths, "Father, forgive them."

The Sadducee walks away. John, Mary, the mother of Jesus, Mary of Magdala, and the other Mary get as close to the foot of the cross as the Roman soldiers will allow. Tears fill my eyes—what must His mother be feeling. She falls to her knees, her face is buried in her hands, and she is sobbing uncontrollably. John kneels beside her and looks dazed, shaking his head in disbelief at the sight of Jesus hanging there on the cross. Mary Magdalene and Mary, the wife of Jesus' uncle Cleophas, each has their hand on Mary's shoulder to comfort her, but they are sobbing, too.

Jesus watches them for a few minutes until Mary looks up at Him. He looks from Mary to John. "Woman, behold your son." He shifts His gaze to John. "Behold your mother." Mary covers her mouth but still lets out a grief-choked wail. She collapses into John's arms.

I scan the crowd looking for familiar faces, especially for those of the apostles. Some of those who have been following Jesus throughout His ministry are scattered among the spectators, but I do not see any of The Twelve except for John. Where can they be? The last time I saw Andrew, he was following Judas to find Caiphas. Did they get arrested? And where is Peter?

James and Judah, the brothers of Jesus, are in the midst of the crowd but nowhere close to their mother. When James and I meet eyes, he nods in acknowledgment but quickly glances away. I wonder if they heard what Jesus just told Mary and John. If Jesus was as perfect a child as He is a man, it must have been hard growing up and being compared to Him. Maybe that is why they are jealous and not followers of Him.

Bartimaeus, the man excommunicated from the synagogue after Jesus healed his blindness, stands at the edge of the crowd keeping a safe distance from the ruling elders. He cringes as he witnesses the Pharisees and Sadducees continuing to throw insults at Jesus, shakes his head, and quickly turns and walks away.

Suddenly, the noon sun is hidden behind black, thick, ominous clouds—it is so dark that the torches must be lit. Many of those watching the crucifixion run for cover, thinking a storm is approaching. Others are still intent on watching Jesus die.

Since the Roman soldiers have the authority to take the clothing of the crucified for themselves, several of the Roman guards are casting lots to determine who gets Jesus' bloodied robe. I guess it must be the thrill of winning because I do not know why anyone would want the blood-soaked robe. The Roman guard who wins the robe holds it high like a prized possession.

Mary pays no attention to the guard's celebration and clutches her chest as she watches her son slip in and out of consciousness. Jesus' breathing is labored, and He tries to reposition His body in order to take a deeper breath. Flies swarm around Him and crawl into His bleeding and open wounds. His body shakes and convulses from dehydration. He cries out hoarsely. "My God, My God, why have You forsaken Me?"

I recognize the Psalm and begin reciting it. "Why are You so far from helping me?" Jesus turns His head, looks at me, and His swollen, dried, chapped lips curl at the ends into a smile. I am overwhelmed with emotion and sink to my knees. I can only mouth the words for the remainder of the psalm as Joseph and others in the crowd complete the recitation.

I jerk as a hand touches my shoulder. Abba kneels beside me, and I lean on him for support as I stand.

Jesus can barely speak because His mouth is so dry. He gasps for air. "I thirst."

Immediately one of the guards fills a sponge from a nearby bucket of stale wine for the Roman guards, puts it on a hyssop branch, and raises it to Jesus' mouth. Jesus lifts His head and looks upward into the dark sky. "It is...finished."

He can hardly breathe, so He pushes up with His feet one more time. "Father...into Your hands...I commend My spirit."

He catches one last shallow breath. His body goes limp, and His head falls forward onto His chest.

His mother screams.

Six hours after Jesus is put on the cross, He is dead. Some in the crowd beat their breasts and tear their robes in mourning. Some shout in victory that the blasphemer is finally dead—especially the Sanhedrin and Pharisees. The ground begins to violently shake. Rocks begin to split, crumble, and fall. People are yelling and running down the hill—tripping and falling over each other in the darkness, trying to enter the safety of the city's walls. A few of us remain at the site. The quake stops.

The centurion does not think anyone hears him, but I do. "Truly, this Man was the Son of God." He looks at me, turns away, and barks orders, "Break their legs! You know they cannot be hanging on the cross on the Jewish Sabbath. It is only three hours away." With their legs broken, they cannot push themselves up to get air and will almost immediately suffocate.

Swinging a large club around his head, the guard walks up to the cross of the first criminal. I cringe at the crunch when the club meets his shins. The man on the cross hardly has enough air to scream as his legs buckle under him, and his arms fully extend, bearing the weight of his body. He quickly succumbs. After seeing and hearing the agony of the crucified criminal, the second one begs for mercy. With no regard or remorse, the guard approaches the second criminal and repeats the process. He approaches Jesus and sees that He is already dead. To make sure, he takes a spear and rams it into Jesus' side under His ribs—there is no reaction from Jesus. When he removes the spear, blood and water gush out.

I feel weak and have a tightness in my chest. My legs are shaky and wobbly. Abba helps me to slowly sit on the ground and squats beside me. I rest my head on my knees. "Jesus is dead. The Messiah is dead."

I feel numb and am not even aware that Benjamin, Micah, and Seba are standing beside me until Benjamin speaks. "He was an amazing Man, and you did what you thought was right. You should have no regrets."

Micah and Benjamin help me to my feet. "Let's go to the house. You and Joseph must be tired after being up all night. And hungry."

I am mentally, physically, and emotionally exhausted, and my head is pounding with each heartbeat. The thought of food is nauseating. "I need to go speak to Mary and John before we leave."

I take a deep breath as I approach them at the foot of the cross, but my voice cracks when I start to speak. I cannot hold back the tears when I look at Mary. Her eyes are almost swollen shut as she stares with a mother's adoration at her dead son on the cross. She can barely catch her breath between sobs. She is leaning on John for support, and he does not look much better. All I can do is embrace her and John at the same time because none of us can talk. We stand in silence for a while, and her eyes never leave the cross. She gives me an understanding nod and squeezes my hand as I turn away.

I look back one more time at Jesus hanging on the cross. I feel hands grabbing me as I become lightheaded and stagger. I see stars. Everything goes black.

# THE REUNION

I wake up on a cot and look around. It takes a moment for me to recognize where I am—alone inside Micah's house. I sit up, stretch, and slowly stand up. I feel weak but walk to the open door and lean against it. The mid-day sun is shining brightly, and I shade my eyes to see where everyone is.

Mother runs to me. "He's awake."

Abba is only a step behind her, and both embrace me tightly. "You had us worried, son. Sit down and let me get you something to eat and drink." Mother runs inside.

I sit in the shade of the fig tree. "Where is everyone?"

"They have gone to the Temple." Abba sits in front of me.

"The Temple? What day is it?"

"It is the Sabbath. You have been out for a while. Benjamin, Micah, and I had to pick you up and bring you here. Joseph was exhausted, too, but he was able to walk home with Seba's help. Neither one of you had eaten or drank anything since the Passover meal."

Tears come to my eyes as I remember Jesus on the cross, but I brush them away as Mother brings me a bowl of chicken stew with matzah. "Eat slowly now."

I break a piece of matzah and dip it in the broth. My mouth waters while I wait for it to get soggy. When it touches my tongue, it melts away. I savor each mouthful of stew and matzah until I consume it all. "Thank you, Mother. That was delicious and just what I needed. I feel much better."

As Mother takes my bowl and I lean against the trunk of the tree, the remainder of the family arrives from the Temple. Benjamin scruffs my hair as he walks by. "I am glad to see you are looking better."

"Thank you. Rest and some food seemed to do the trick. How was Temple?"

Joseph sits beside me. "About the time Jesus died yesterday, the parochet was ripped from top to bottom."

I raise my eyebrows. "The veil to the Holy of Holies was torn? How? Who would do that?"

"Rumors are it looked as if someone, or something, grabbed the curtain and pulled it apart. Many think it was Yahweh, but the priests are blaming it on the earthquake. Their theory does not seem plausible since The Temple had no other damage."

Joseph leans over and speaks just above a whisper. "I met Joab at the Temple."

"Who?"

"The owner of the house where Jesus and the apostles had Passover. Some of the apostles are hiding out there—he would not say who is there. But they are still afraid the Romans are going to arrest Jesus' followers. They told Joab to let us know where they are if we want to visit, but we must be careful not to be followed or let anyone see us."

"We need to go. Andrew and Peter might be there." I try to stand, but Abba pulls me back down.

"Until you regain all your strength, you are staying here. You can go later. In fact, both of you may need to keep a low profile, too."

Turning to Abba, I take a deep breath and open my mouth to argue, but I know he is right. "Maybe we can go later this afternoon."

I must have been more tired than I thought because I wake up still leaning against the tree as the sun is setting. Clop... Clop... Clop goes the sound of horse hoofs on the street. Two Roman soldiers look my way as they pass the opening to the courtyard. When it sounds like they are down the street, I peek around the wall to see what they are doing. They stop just past the house where the apostles are hiding and turn around. They trot in my direction, then pick up speed to a gallop and pass the entrance and out of hearing distance. Whew... that was unnerving.

Abba stands up as I enter the house. "What is the matter, Son? Your hands are trembling."

When I tell them what happened, Abba tells me Benjamin and Joseph are about to carry some food to Joab's house. "I am not sure that is such a good idea now, fellows."

Benjamin walks outside and quickly returns. "The streets are clear. We will be careful." He picks up a basket of smoked fish and bread, and Joseph grabs a pouch filled with fruit and vegetables. They both look at me, and all three of us shift our gaze to Abba.

Abba strokes his beard and takes a deep breath. "I know you want to go, Matthias, and I am not going to stand in your way. It is your decision."

I jump to my feet, hug him, and turn toward the door. "Let's go."

Although the sun has set, it is still bright enough to see without using a torch. The brief walk to Joab's home is uneventful—there is no one on the street. When Benjamin knocks on the door, a short, plump man opens it slowly. "Shalom, and welcome." When we enter, he closes and bolts the door behind us. "We can't be too careful."

When Benjamin introduces me to him, Joab grabs my arm and shakes it. "I heard a lot about you from these two earlier today...and from some of our mutual friends." He motions with his head toward the steps leading upstairs. "Follow me. I'm sure your friends will be glad to see you."

At the top of the stairs, Joab knocks on another locked door. "You have some welcome guests. It is safe to open the door."

The hinges squeak as the heavy wooden door opens wide enough for someone inside to peer out. I recognize the swollen red eyes—Peter. He sobs as he grabs me by the shoulders and pulls me close for a tight embrace. He pushes me away but keeps one hand behind my neck, so we can look into each other's eyes. "Forgive me. I am such a coward. Not only did I abandon and deny knowing our Messiah, but I left you...all of you...to defend yourselves. And now I am hiding behind locked doors." He gets down on one knee. "Please forgive me."

"Get up, Peter. We all abandoned Him...not just you. We all ran away and left Jesus alone to face the Roman torture."

"But you were at the cross. I have stayed in hiding since the other night." Peter stands but keeps his head down. His tears fall on the floor. "I should have been there, too."

I do not know what to say to comfort him. "It is probably better you stay in hiding for a while. After all, you did cut off the ear of the servant of Caiphas."

He lifts his head and has a half-smile as he proudly puffs out his chest and walks away. "Yes, I did, didn't I?"

I look around the large room for the first time to see who is there. In one corner, Andrew is talking to Joseph, Benjamin, and Joab. Mary, the mother of Jesus, is crying on John's shoulder at the large table where Jesus and the apostles probably had the Passover meal. John waves to me, but his face has no expression. Seated on cushions close to Jesus' mother is Mary of Magdala, Jesus' aunt Mary, and Joanna, who had followed Jesus after He had healed her. On the other side of John sits his mother, Salome, then James, and Zebedee. Simon, the zealot, is standing, gripping his sword, and staring out the window. Several men are asleep on the floor in the other corner and have the hoods of their robes covering their faces; I am not sure who they are.

Peter quickly returns. "Did you hear? Judas killed himself."

I take a step back and shake my head in denial. "No. The last time I saw him, he was frantically looking for Caiphas. He was trying to stop the crucifixion."

"As you know, he did not stop that from happening. The guilt of betraying the Messiah must have been too much for him to handle, and he hanged himself. Supposedly, Judas tried to return the money he received for betraying Jesus to the elders in the Temple...."

"Yes, I remember him holding a bag of coins."

"Since those coins were 'the price for blood,' the elders did not want to keep them, so they are buying a potter's field to bury strangers."

"I guess his death will not go in vain, but I can't believe he killed himself." I squat down, shaking my head, trying to regain my composure.

Peter kneels beside me. "Tell me everything that happened after I denied knowing Jesus and ran away. I want to know every detail... since I missed most of it. I have asked John when Mary is not with him, but he has been so busy comforting her, he has not had time to talk to me. You and Joseph are the only other ones who were there the whole time."

I look at the open window and see the darkness outside, wondering if I should stay. "It is going to take a while to tell you everything."

"All I have is time. Please. Sit and tell me."

We sit on the floor next to a torch in the corner of the room. Peter pulls his knees to his chest and rests his chin on his arms. Benjamin and Joseph walk over. "Are you ready to go? We need to get back to the house. It is dark outside, and I know the family is concerned, especially your parents."

Peter sighs and lays his head down on his arms but looks up when I put my hand on his shoulder. "I am going to stay here tonight. Peter wants me to tell him everything that happened. I will be there early in the morning."

Benjamin squats beside me to get a better look at my shadowed face. "Are you feeling well enough for that?"

"Thank you for being concerned, but I am fine."

Joab escorts Benjamin and Joseph out but soon returns and bolts the door behind him. Peter extinguishes the burning torch and replaces it with an oil lamp while Philip replaces Simon, the Zealot, at the window.

I hope that Mary cannot hear me as I tell Peter everything that happened, including the gruesome details. An occasional whimper comes from her direction as our conversation goes well into the night.

# UNBELIEVABLE NEWS

It must be a little before sunrise as I awaken to the whisper of Mary of Magdala, Salome, Joanna, and Jesus' aunt as they ask Joab to let them leave. "We need to go anoint the body of Jesus with the oils and spices."

Although Joab is reluctant about letting the women go alone, the door to the upper room is unbolted, and the door creeks open. The women slip out as Joab leads them down the steps. The main door is unlocked and within seconds is relocked. Joab bolts the upstairs door when he reenters the room.

I join Cleopas, Jesus' uncle, at the open window. He holds his index finger to his lips for me to be quiet as we watch his wife Mary and the other women weave their way through people who are already going to the Temple for dedication of the first fruits of the spring harvest to God—it is the Day of Resheet and the end of winter. The first sheaf of green barley from the harvest is taken to the priest to wave before the Lord as a gesture of dedication to Him, and an unblemished lamb is sacrificed as a burnt offering, and only after the ceremony is complete can the crop be used.

He whispers as we lose sight of the women, "Go back to sleep. We may need you to stand guard later."

I obey.

"Quick! Let them in!" Cleopas bellows as he runs toward the bolted door. "The women are running up the street!"

Everyone in the room jumps to their feet and follows Joab downstairs. Several have swords in their hands as he opens the door, and the women run inside breathless. He quickly bolts the door behind them. "What's wrong?"

Mary of Magdala is gasping for breath and holding her chest. She pushes the words out. "He has risen from the grave...Jesus is alive!"

Luckily, John is standing nearby and catches Mary, the mother of Jesus, as her body goes limp into his arms. She regains her balance, stands, and looks hopefully into the faces of each of the women. She brushes away the tears streaming down her cheeks. "Please tell me this is not a rumor, and my Jesus is alive."

The women nod, and while they catch their breath, Salome does all the talking. "As we approached the tomb, we were concerned about who would roll the stone away from the opening. The Roman guards were nowhere in sight when we got there, but the stone was already moved. When we peeped in, there were two men clothed in long white robes sitting at the head and feet where His body was laid, but His body was not there. Of course, we screamed. They told us to not be afraid and asked why we were seeking the living among the dead. Before any of us could answer, one of them said, 'He is not here but is risen.' The other one reminded us of what Jesus said— how He must be delivered into the hands of sinful men, be crucified, and the third day He would rise again. Today is the third day. Before they vanished from our sight, they commanded us to go and tell His disciples. We immediately came here as quickly as we could."

Not believing what we have just been told, some of the apostles start asking questions.

"Who were these men?"

"Who rolled the stone away?"

"Did someone steal His body? Where did they take Him?"

Peter holds his hand up and commands everyone to be quiet and stop asking questions. He turns to Mary of Magdala. "Take me there. I have been too scared to show my face since He was betrayed, but I want to see the empty tomb. Take me there, now!" I am glad Peter seems to be back to his old self and taking charge. "Everyone else, remain here where it is safe. We will be back as soon as possible."

Jesus' mother tells John to go with Peter and Mary of Magdala as they cautiously exit the house. Joab bolts the door behind them as the rest of us ascend the steps to our refuge. We wait anxiously for their arrival, but time drags.

When Cleopas hollers, "They are back," we almost trample Joab after he unbolts the door. We rush down the steps and start asking questions before Peter, John, and Mary of Magdala can enter the house.

"What did you find at the tomb?"

"Where is the body?"

"What did you see?"

Once safe inside and the door closed and locked, John begins. "We ran to the tomb, and I arrived first. I stooped and peered into the tomb and saw the linen clothes lying there but waited for Peter. He pushed me aside when he got there, and I followed him inside."

Peter smiles and pats John's shoulder. "I am sorry I pushed you, John, but I could not wait to see inside. When I entered the tomb, the linen clothes were neatly folded in a place by themselves. The handkerchief that covered His face was in a different place on the stone slab." He looks at Mary. "There was no trace of Jesus' body or the two men in white."

Mary winces and swallows hard. Tears fill her eyes as she glances at each face of those who went to the tomb. Peter sees her disappointment and hugs her tightly. "We can only hope what the two men told the women is true—that Jesus is alive and risen from the dead."

The face of Jesus' mother lights up when Mary of Magdala proclaims, "It is true. While I waited in the garden. I thought the man approaching me was the gardener. I asked him where the body was taken, and He called me by name. Immediately. I knew it was Jesus and reached to hug Him, but He stepped back and wouldn't let me touch Him. He said He had not yet ascended to the Father."

Cleopas and his wife Mary tell Joab they need to go to Emmaus to tell their family about the latest news but will return tomorrow with victuals for everyone. I should do the same but do not want to leave here yet. I will go tell my family the news later.

I want to talk to Peter alone and see what he believes happened to the body. But I do not get that chance.

# THE APPEARANCE

Knock...knock...knock!

We stand quietly and motionless—afraid to move. Swords are slowly unsheathed, and weapons appear in the hands of most of the apostles. The women slowly move upstairs.

Knock...knock...knock!

A voice just above a whisper is heard from the other side of the door. "Joab, it's Benjamin, Jesse, and Joseph."

Whew...I take a deep breath.

The door is opened, and Abba, Benjamin, and Joseph are holding two baskets and a bag probably filled with fresh fruit and vegetables. My mouth waters as I catch a whiff of the freshly baked bread and the broiled fish. "We saw three of you run past the gate. We were ready to intercept anyone following you, but we did not want to holler at you in case you were in danger. Is everyone safe?"

"We are fine." Peter begins recounting the morning's events to them as Abba gives Joab the basket of fish and approaches me. Abba freezes in place when he hears Jesus' body is missing. Abba glances at Benjamin and Joseph and then at me but says nothing until the food is taken to the upper room and is spread on the table for those who want to eat.

As I grab a piece of fish and some bread, Abba pulls me aside and hugs me. "Let's go over here." Joseph and Benjamin follow, and we all sit in an empty corner. "What do you think happened to the body, son? Who do you think would steal it?"

I lean against the cold stone wall and stare at his troubled expression before answering. "I honestly do not know what to believe. We have seen Him do some unbelievable things, and everything He ever told us would happen has occurred. He predicted all of this would happen and said He would be raised from the dead on the third day. Today is the third day, and His body is not in the tomb.

Who would steal His body?" I shrug. "After being tortured to the extent He was and crucified, He truly is the Son of God if He is alive. However, I just do not see how He can be alive. That would be impossible, wouldn't it?"

Abba looks at me sadly. "I know you want to believe—we all do. But after seeing Him hanging dead on the cross, I think it is impossible for Him to be alive today. Why don't you come back to the house with us and get some rest? You have had a rough couple of days."

"I will shortly. I want to talk to Peter some more before I go back."

By now, all the apostles except Thomas have reunited in the upper room. It is the middle of the afternoon, and they have been sharing stories and rumors about followers being taken captive by the Roman soldiers. Strategies are being discussed and debated whether everyone should remain together or split into smaller groups, pairs, or go out individually. Are we safer as a group or individually? No one knows.

A knock on the door... Andrew leans out the window to see who is there. "It's Cleopas and Mary. What are they doing back so soon?"

Something must have happened. They said they would not be back until tomorrow.

They rush inside when the door is opened. Cleopas wife runs to the mother of Jesus and holds her at arms' length. "We saw Him! He is alive!"

Mary's legs buckle, but Cleopas catches her, and she regains her balance. "We were on the road and talking among ourselves when a man joined us. We did not recognize him. I do not know why I felt comfortable enough to honestly answer him when he asked what we were talking about. I asked if he had not heard about the events in Jerusalem concerning Jesus of Nazareth. About His trial and crucifixion and our hope that He was our Messiah. I told him about the women finding the empty tomb and the two angels appearing to them and telling them He is alive."

"We should have known immediately who He was by His response, but we didn't. He said, 'Ought not the Christ to have suffered these things and to enter into His glory?' He then began at Moses and the Prophets and expounded about all the prophecies concerning the Messiah."

Everyone glances around but remains quiet. My mind is racing. Was it really Jesus?

Cleopas' wife takes advantage of the moment of silence. "He sat down to eat with us, and He took the bread, lifted it toward Heaven, blessed it, broke it, and gave it to us. Our eyes were immediately opened. We knew it was Jesus, but then He vanished from our sight."

I look around the room at everyone's stunned expressions. Mary, the mother of Jesus, has a broad smile on her face and is squeezing the wife of Cleopas. There are whispers among some and shaking of heads in disbelief. Several others raise eyebrows in doubt as they look at each other.

*I do not know what to believe. I saw His mutilated body hanging on the cross and the sword jabbed in His side. He was dead. How could He now be alive?*

My thoughts are interrupted by "Shalom Aleichem. Peace to you." A body dressed in a snow-white robe is standing in our midst. If the door had been unlocked, several would have run out because they are cowered against the wall. There are a few shrieks of fear. I fall onto my wobbly knees as I look at the face. The facial features are those of Jesus. His complexion is the same color but seems to have a slight glow. His eyes meet mine, and He smiles. That is Jesus' smile. I cannot believe what I am seeing. Jesus is standing in front of me, or I think He is. I stare in disbelief. How?

He looks around the room. "Why are you troubled? Why do you have doubts?"

No one answers.

He spreads His arms to reveal the imprints of the nails in His hands then points to His feet. "Behold my hands and feet. Come, touch, and see. A spirit does not have flesh and bones as you see I have."

His mother slowly approaches Him with arms outstretched. With quivering hands, she gently touches His face, then pulls Him close and kisses His cheeks. He wipes away her tears of joy and hugs her tightly. They cling to each other for a while until He tenderly pushes her away.

Peter is next. He throws his arms around Jesus' neck and weeps on His shoulder. "Master... please forgive me for denying You... I swore I would not deny You...but I was a coward and scared...not only did I deny You... I denied You three times... I ran away and hid... I could not face anyone... I am so sorry... please forgive me."

Jesus wraps His arms around Peter and lets him cry for a moment. "Peter, look at me."

Peter lifts his tear-filled eyes and looks into the eyes of Jesus. "Peter, your sins are forgiven and washed clean by my blood that was shed on the cross."

"Thank you, Master...thank you." Peter embraces Him and wipes away his tears on the sleeve of his robe. He slowly backs away, not taking his eyes off Jesus.

John, James, and Andrew eagerly approach Jesus and hug Him. The other apostles are more cautious and unsure but still greet Him with love and affection. Behind them are Cleopas and his wife and Joab.

I am next. What do I do?

I cannot control the tears as they run into my beard. I fall at His feet, barely touching where the spike was hammered into it three days ago. It is real. He touches me on the shoulder, and I gaze into His face as He squats in front of me. "Yes, it is I. I am."

I sob.

He helps me to my feet and hugs me before Peter comes and walks me away. It takes me a while to regain my composure, but now I have no doubt. This is not just an apparition. I touched Him. He touched me. Jesus rose from the grave and is a live human being. He is the Son of God. He is alive!

When Jesus finishes personally greeting everyone in the room, He asks for food. Joab gives Him a piece of the broiled fish that Abba brought and some honeycomb. He devours it quickly as everyone silently eyes Him closely. A spirit cannot do that. He is real.

He faces everyone. "These are My words I spoke to you while I was with you—that everything written about Me in the Law of Moses, the Prophets, and the Psalms must be fulfilled."

He explains the Scriptures so we can fully comprehend the importance and relationships of all of the prophecies concerning Him. "To fulfill prophecies, I was conceived by the Holy Spirit and born of a virgin in the town of Bethlehem, the place where the lambs are born to be sacrificed at the Temple in Jerusalem for the Passover. I am a descendant of Abraham, the father to all Jews, and King David through my earthly father Joseph and my mother, Mary."

"A messenger, John the Baptist, prepared the way for Me and My ministry. I brought the Light to Galilee, healed the sick and brokenhearted, and taught in parables. As Zechariah proclaimed, I made a triumphal entry into Jerusalem on a donkey and was betrayed by one of my followers for thirty pieces of silver—that money would be used to buy a potter's field. I died by crucifixion with my hands and feet pierced by spikes. Although I did not receive royal treatment, I was called a king—King of the Jews."

"Isaiah proclaimed I would be tried and condemned, smitten and spat upon, but remain silent before my accusers. My cross stood in between the crosses of two criminals fulfilling the prophecy I would suffer and die with sinners."

"When I cried out to My Father asking why He had forsaken Me, those of you at the cross finished reciting the Psalm of David that describes the scene at the cross." He looks at me and smiles.

"Like the Passover lamb, I died as a sin offering for mankind as Isaiah foretold, and it was necessary for the Christ to suffer and to rise from the dead on the third day that repentance and remission of sins should be preached in His name to all nations, beginning at Jerusalem. Today is the third day, and here I am. Alive and standing in your midst."

"You are witnesses of these things. Behold, I send the Promise of My Father upon you, but tarry in the city of Jerusalem until you are endued with power from on high."

Before anyone has time to comment or ask questions about when that is going to happen, Jesus disappears into thin air. Someone asks the question anyway, while everyone else sits dumbfounded, unsure of what to do next. Peter stands. "We wait here in Jerusalem just like He said. Jesus is alive. He will not leave us alone for long. He will return and tell us what to do next."

Jesus' mother brushes away a tear as she walks away from the group toward the corner of the room. Since she has seen her son, she seems lost in thought but has a slight smile. Her posture is upright and straight, unlike the hump-shouldered, sobbing woman she was only a few hours ago. She does not look like a grieving mother now—and is not. Her son is alive.

# SPREADING THE NEWS

I must go and tell my family the news. Joab locks the door behind me, and I cautiously exit the gate as the sun is setting over the city. As I merge into the crowded street, my heart races as two Roman soldiers slowly pass. As they move away, my pace quickens until I reach the safety of the home of Micah and Nava.

When I round the corner into the courtyard, Mother and Elizabeth are removing some loaves of freshly baked unleavened bread from the outdoor oven. "That smells delicious." They jerk their heads around and yelp as I hug both of them.

Mother gives me a loving swat. "You scared us, son."

"Have I got some unbelievable news for the family. Let's go inside."

They gather the loaves of bread and follow me inside. I am greeted by hugs from everyone. Benjamin pats me on the shoulder. "Any word on the missing body, Matthias? How is everyone at Joab's?"

Everyone sits. "First, everyone is doing well at Joab's. And there is word on the body, but I will get to that later. Since you already know about the discovery of the empty tomb, I will skip that part."

"Please do. I want to know where they found the body. And who took it." Joseph puts his hands on his nervously bouncing knees as if to keep them still and stares intently at me.

"After Peter, John, and Mary of Magdala returned from the tomb and told about the grave cloths, Cleopas and his wife left for Emmaus and were planning to return tomorrow with food for everyone. This was before the three of you came. Not long ago, they returned unexpectedly with some news. Jesus appeared to them on the road."

Among the gasps are questions and comments of disbelief.

After I tell them their whole story and that He vanished from their sight, everyone sighs as if disappointed by Jesus' disappearance and begins to stand and walk away. Benjamin puts his hand on my shoulder. "Sounds like they let their imagination get the best of them."

I shake my head. "No, wait. Sit back down. You do not understand. That is not all of the story." They slowly return to their seats...I think just to pacify me.

"That was the way most of us in the room felt. Although there were small pockets of whispering, no one said anything out loud. We all wanted to believe, but the story seemed too far-fetched."

Seba nods his head. "Yes, it is. I must agree with Benjamin. It sounds like the heat got to them, and they were seeing things."

"When you hear the rest of the story, I think your opinions will change."

I pause to gather my thoughts before continuing. "While we were standing around not knowing what to think, a body suddenly appeared in the middle of the room." I look at Seba as he shakes his head and looks at Abba. "The locked room."

"Since the door was locked, no one could leave, but some got as close to the walls as they could. He greeted us with 'Shalom,' and when I looked at His face, my legs buckled, and I fell to my knees. His smile. His eyes. It was Jesus."

I do not like what I see as I scan the faces of my family. They are the faces I saw when Arat died. They are faces of pity for me. Tears are welling in my mother's eyes. Abba's gaze quickly shifts toward the door as our eyes meet. My parents do not believe me—no one does.

"I know this sounds crazy, but it is true. You can ask anyone that was in that room."

No one will look me in the face. Joseph has his head lowered and is picking at his thumbnail. Benjamin and Seba are both looking in my direction, but not into my eyes. When I look at him, Micah shifts his gaze to Nava, who is staring at the ground. Elizabeth is leaning over, patting Mother on the knee while Martha holds Mother's hand.

"He asked why we were scared and did not believe. He showed us the wounds from the spikes in His hands and His feet and told us to come touch and see for ourselves. His mother was the first. She hugged and kissed Him. We all took turns. I fell at His feet sobbing. I even touched where the nail went into His foot. He was real. He even ate a piece of the fish that you brought over."

I take a deep breath before saying anything else. I know I am sounding desperate, and what I am saying is falling on deaf ears. What can I do or say to convince them I am telling the truth? I turn and walk toward the door.

I spin around and walk toward Benjamin. My face feels like it is on fire, and my eyes are watery. He flinches when I get close, and I point at him. "Benjamin, you have been a believer from the beginning. Come with me to Joab's house and ask him or anyone there what happened." I point around the room as everyone stares at me. "Then come tell them what everyone experienced there. Maybe they will believe you. They sure do not believe me."

I do not wait for his or anyone else response and almost run outside. My head is pounding. Why won't anyone believe me? I hear footsteps behind me as I exit the gate but do not turn around.

"Wait! We will go with you." I take a quick look over my shoulder, and Abba, Benjamin, and Joseph are running toward me.

I only slow down long enough to ensure there are no Roman soldiers around as I rush out the gate onto the crowded street. "Wait, son!" is the last thing I hear until I get to the door to Joab's house.

Joab opens the door as Abba, Benjamin, and Joseph arrive, and we hurry inside. "Joab, they do not believe me. Please tell them what happened here today after they left, so they will not think I have lost my mind."

As I am sitting on the cushion next to Joab, the mother of Jesus places her hand on my shoulder. "He told you the truth. Believe him." She walks away.

Abba's chin trembles as the color leaves his face. Benjamin tugs at his beard as he drops his chin to his chest. Joseph pulls his legs up to his chest and buries his face. They could not look me in the face a while ago because they felt sorry for me. Now they can't because they are feeling sorry for themselves for not believing me.

Joab quickly begins describing the return of Cleopas and his wife and their experience on the road to Emmaus. "We all had our doubts Jesus was alive until He suddenly appeared in the middle of the group. We saw the nail prints in His hands and feet—some of us even touched them." He looks at me and winks. From the corner of my eye, I see Abba's chest heave and hear him muffle a sob. Benjamin reaches over and pats him on the leg.

"Jesus asked if we had any food, so I gave Him a piece of the fish you brought and a honeycomb. When He finished eating, He began teaching us about what Moses and the Prophets wrote about the Messiah." Joab gives an unbelievably detailed account of what was said and concludes with Jesus' command to stay in Jerusalem until we receive the power from on high. Jesus then vanished from our sight.

Abba sobs. "Please forgive me...for not believing you, Matthias. The story is so unbelievable... I thought you had returned to that dark hole you were in...when you lost Arat...and your son." He grabs me and buries his face into my shoulder.

Benjamin hugs us both. "We all thought that. Forgive us."

"I am sorry, too." Joseph pats me on the shoulder. "What do we do now?"

A booming voice from behind me answers. It is Peter. "We wait here like Jesus said to do."

Abba must think he cannot apologize enough for doubting me as we stroll on the moonlit street back to the home of Micah and Nava. Plus, he is clinging to me like a lost child.

We enter the house, and Elizabeth is trying to comfort my crying mother. When Mother looks at me, she sobs. I squat beside her and take her hand. "Mother, everything is fine. I will let Abba tell you what happened." I want to add, "Maybe all of you will believe him," but decide that is better left unsaid.

Abba motions for everyone to sit. "Everyone, please gather around. I want all of you to hear what I have to say." He looks at Benjamin and Joseph. "Feel free to interrupt at any time you want to add anything."

He puts his hand on my shoulder. "I, like everyone else in here, thought Matthias had returned to the dark hole he was in when Arat and the baby died. I apologize again for not believing you, Matthias. Please forgive me."

Mother glances around as if looking for answers as I pat his hand and smile. "For the hundredth time, Abba, you are forgiven."

Abba sees the confusion on Mother's face. "When we entered Joab's house, Matthias immediately told him to tell us what happened—his family did not believe him. Jesus' mother was standing there and put her hand on Matthias' shoulder and told us to believe him, turned, and walked away. Only a few hours earlier, she was a frail grieving mother, but she was now a confident and happy individual. I knew at that moment Matthias had told us the truth. I was devastated for not believing you, Matthias—I still am. Joab began describing the events exactly as Matthias had told us. Each person in the room hugged Jesus."

Mother begins to cry and wraps her arms around my neck. "I am sorry I did not believe you, son."

"It's fine, Mother. The story is unbelievable. I am not sure I would believe it if I had not been there to experience it."

Abba waits until Mother stops crying before he continues. "Joab continued to describe the events where Matthias stopped—or we stopped him. He said Jesus ate with them and then gave a detailed summary of the prophecies He had fulfilled as our Messiah."

Benjamin interrupts. "That is why it took so long. Joab told us each of the prophecies Jesus fulfilled. It was time-consuming but highly informative."

Abba looks at Benjamin to make sure he is finished speaking. "Jesus commanded them to remain in Jerusalem until they receive the power from on high. He then vanished into thin air."

"Let me get this straight. Jesus had a physical body that could be touched? You said you touched it, Matthias?"

"Yes. I did touch Him, and He touched me, Seba."

"But He can magically appear in a locked room and also vanish into thin air. How?"

"That is one of the mysteries of God. How did Jesus perform any of the miracles we saw? I cannot explain any of them, but they happened. All I know is Jesus overcame the grave and is alive today. I have seen Him. I have touched Him."

Everyone sits quietly, pondering what they have heard. One by one, they each apologize to me for ever doubting what I told them.

I am thankful I am not in the condition they thought I was. Thank you, God.

# SIGHTINGS

The Passover week festivities are ending, and Benjamin, Elizabeth, Abba, Mother, Seba, and Martha must leave early in the morning to return to Bethsaida. They are inside, gathering their things for the long journey home.

"We have not talked about it, Joseph, but have you decided whether you are going home or staying in Jerusalem?"

"I don't know yet. I know it is not possible, but I wish I could be in both places. The family needs us at home, but Jesus commanded us to stay here. What are you going to do?"

"Like you, I would like to be in both places, too. It has been a joy to be around our family so much these last few days, and I hate to not go home with them, but we have experienced too much to go home now. I am staying in Jerusalem like Jesus said."

"I knew that is what you would do without asking. I wish I was so decisive."

"You better decide soon since they are leaving in the morning."

"I know. I need to think about it some more. I am torn and not sure what to do."

"It is a win-win situation. Just follow your heart, Joseph." I walk inside.

The sun is barely above the horizon as Joseph and I walk the family to the city gate. Abba apologizes to me again as he envelops me in his arms one last time. Mother kisses my cheek and, with a quivering chin, tells me she loves me. Although we have not seen Jesus since the day after the Sabbath, Joseph and I have both decided to stay in Jerusalem as Jesus told us. Micah and Nava ask us to stay with them, but we accept Joab's offer to stay at his house with the apostles in case Jesus makes another appearance there.

When we enter Joab's home, Matthew is reporting to those gathered. "I heard from a very reliable source; the Sanhedrin held an impromptu meeting to refute the news of Jesus' resurrection circulating throughout Jerusalem and the surrounding area. They have paid the Roman guards who were guarding the tomb a sizeable sum of money to spread lies about the disappearance of Jesus' body. Instead of telling how there was an earthquake, and they ran away in fear as an angel descended from the clouds and rolled away the stone blocking the tomb's entrance, the guards are spreading the rumor that while they were asleep during the night, we stole his body." We all laugh at how ridiculous that story sounds, and he concludes. "I guess they were sound sleepers."

"They must have been paid a substantial amount. A Roman guard would not ever want to admit to sleeping on his watch. It is a capital offense."

What a conniving group of men who are supposed to be our religious leaders. The Sanhedrin will stop at nothing.

Unfortunately, I only see Jesus three times over the next forty days:

Eight days after His initial appearance in the upper room, Jesus appears in the middle of the locked room again. Joseph is here to see Him this time...and so is Thomas, the only apostle who was not with us at the first sighting. Like the initial response of my family, Thomas does not believe what he has been told we saw.

"Shalom."

Although everyone except Joseph and Thomas has witnessed this before, the shock is still there. Everyone steps back a couple of steps, except Thomas. With eyes widening and his mouth falling open, Thomas backs into the corner as quickly and as far away as he can. He shields his face with his hands as Jesus slowly walks toward him.

"Don't be afraid, Thomas. Reach your finger here and look at My hands. Reach your hand and thrust it into My side. Do not be unbelieving but believe."

Trembling, Thomas crumples to the floor with his face at Jesus' feet. He raises his shaking hands toward Jesus, and his voice quivers when he finally speaks. "My Lord and My God."

Jesus kneels beside him and hugs him. "Thomas, because you have seen Me, you have believed. Blessed are those who have not seen and yet have believed."

If for no other reason than for Thomas to hear it from His own mouth, Jesus repeats how the Messiah has fulfilled the Law of Moses and the Prophets. And then He vanishes.

Several days later, Jesus shows Himself again by the Sea of Galilee. We Jews still like to call it that even though the Roman government has renamed it the Sea of Tiberius after the Roman emperor Tiberius Caesar.

Peter decides to go fishing and is joined by the apostles John, James, Thomas, and Nathaniel. Joseph and I jump at the opportunity to go, too. We cautiously leave the confines of Jerusalem to board the ship Peter has procured. We raise the sails and drift out to sea to night-fish. It is nice to be away from the hustle and bustle of Jerusalem, especially the events surrounding this Passover, and at a place where we feel comfortable.

As the sun is setting, we anchor the boat, cast our nets, and wait. No one speaks as we absorb the peace of being on the serene water we are so familiar with. The only sound is the waves lapping at the sides of the boat. The moon soon lights up the night sky, and its reflection glistens on the water. I stare into the blanket of twinkling stars and wonder what is going to be the next phase of this journey before dozing off to a restful nap.

Although we cast the nets on both sides of the ship, the night passes without catching a fish. No one minds. As we approach the shore, a man watching us from the beach asks, "Do you have any meat?"

When we respond that we do not, he shouts, "Cast the net on the right side of the ship, and you will find!"

We all exchange glances as we recollect the mass quantity of fish we caught when Jesus commanded us to do the same. Could that man be Jesus? I look back at the shore. With the hood of his robe partially hiding his face, the morning fog hovering above the water, and the distance we are from shore, it is impossible for me to distinguish any of the man's facial features.

With nothing to lose, we cast the net on the right side of the boat and are not able to draw it in for the multitude of fish. John looks at Peter. "It is the Lord."

Peter grabs his outer garment, dives into the sea, and swims to shore. Although Peter is a strong swimmer, he arrives about the same time we do, pulling the net full of fish behind the boat. As soon as we get close to land, the man already has a fire of coals with some fish on it and some bread. When he tells us to bring some of the fish we have caught, Peter swims over and helps us drag the net to shore. The net is full of one hundred fifty-three large musht.

"Come and dine." The man has enough fish already cooked for us to sit and eat while more are put on the hot coals. We gather around the open fire, and when the man takes the bread and fish and blesses them, there is no doubt it is Jesus.

After we finish eating, Jesus turns to Peter. "Simon, son of Jonas, do you love me more than these?

"Yes, Lord. You know I do."

"Feed my lambs."

You can hear the annoyance in Peter's response when Jesus asks him, not only twice but three times. Jesus then holds His hands outstretched as when He was on the cross and makes an odd comment to Peter. "When older, you will stretch out your hands like this and be taken where you do not want to go. Follow me."

Is Jesus predicting Peter's death? I think that is the way Peter perceives it because he turns and points to John. "What about him?"

"If it is My will he be alive when I come again, what is that to you? Do not worry about him. You, follow Me."

In the blink of an eye, Jesus is gone.

By the fortieth day, we have returned to Jerusalem from our fishing excursion in Galilee. Jesus appears to us in the upper room. Although believers are still being persecuted by the Romans, He leads us through the streets of Jerusalem unnoticed by the people of the city. Of course, the streets are not as crowded as they were during Passover, and there are fewer Roman guards. We exit the eastern gate and walk to Bethany on the eastern slopes of the Mount of Olives.

Jesus does not say anything the whole time we are walking. We stop when He turns and faces us. "It is not for you to know the times or the seasons which the Father has put in His own power. But you shall receive power when the Holy Ghost is upon you. You shall be witnesses of me in Jerusalem, Judaea, Samaria, and to the utmost parts of the earth.

He smiles and raises His hands toward heaven. "All power is given unto Me in heaven and in earth. Now go and teach all nations baptizing them in the name of the Father, and of the Son, and of the Holy Ghost."

He looks taller. No wonder. His feet are not touching the ground. He must be two feet off the ground. What is happening? Slowly, His body begins to ascend. We all take a step back and watch as He continues to rise. He is at least ten feet higher as He looks down upon us. "Teach them to observe all things I have commanded you. Lo, I am with you always, even unto the end of the world."

Falling to my knees, I gaze steadfastly toward heaven until He is lost in the clouds.

Two men dressed in white robes suddenly stand in our midst. "You men of Galilee, why are you gazing up into heaven? This same

Jesus, which is taken up into heaven shall return in like manner as you have seen Him go up."

They disappear as I look back to the last spot I saw Jesus in the clouds...hopefully, to see Him descending. I do not. He is gone.

# THE REPLACEMENT

Little is said on the descent down the slopes of the Mount of Olives to the city until we get to the upper room. Peter stands in the middle of the more than one hundred people who have gathered. Behind him stand the other ten apostles. Where did all these people come from? Did they all witness Jesus' ascension into heaven?

"Brothers and sisters, long ago the Holy Ghost spoke through David concerning Judas Iscariot, who became the guide to those who arrested Jesus. That scripture had to be fulfilled and now has been. He was one of us, one of The Twelve, and had his assigned place in this ministry. Most of you have already heard he purchased a field now called the Field of Blood with the thirty pieces of silver he received for betraying Jesus—the reward for his iniquity. This also fulfills the scriptures. It is written in the book of Psalms, 'Let his habitation be desolate and let no man dwell therein.'

Peter takes a deep breath before continuing, "You have probably also heard Judas Iscariot hanged himself, the rope broke, and he fell headlong to his death, burst open, and all his guts gushed out. I apologize for being so blunt and descriptive, but we are all saddened he felt there was no hope for him, and he resorted to this action." Peter pauses for a moment of silence.

"David also said, 'Let someone else take over his post' when his position is vacated. Which brings us to the business at hand— Judas must now be replaced, so we will number twelve again. His replacement must be one of the men who has accompanied us during the time the Lord Jesus was among us—beginning from the baptism by John until the day Jesus was taken up from us into heaven. He must be ordained to be a witness with us of His resurrection. A decision needs to be made, so excuse us while we talk among ourselves."

Peter turns and huddles with the other apostles to choose someone. Joseph and I talk among ourselves about the ascension. We are interrupted when Peter steps away from the other apostles and faces the crowd to make the announcement.

"We have narrowed it down to two men. I can personally attest that these two men were at the baptism and have been with us throughout Jesus' ministry. They were with us when Jesus was betrayed, and unlike most of the apostles, they were at the foot of the cross at Jesus' crucifixion."

"They were with us the day we received the news of the empty tomb and also witnessed Jesus' ascension into heaven. Because we are having trouble deciding which of these two will be the replacement of Judas, it is going to take more prayer and deliberation because both men are deserving. So all of you know, the two men being considered are...." Peter scans the crowd and stops when he sees us and points. "Joseph and Matthias."

I jerk my head back in shock and gasp for air. I shake my head to clear my thoughts and stare at Peter. I mouth "Me?" because no sound will come out.

Peter laughs and nods his head.

I look at Joseph, and he seems just as surprised at the apostles' decision. He is frozen in place, and his eyes are glazed over as he gazes into space. He blinks rapidly as if coming out of a trance and runs his hand through his hair.

We give each other congratulatory hugs as Andrew comes and pulls us toward the apostles. People pat us on the back as we are led through the crowd. Is this really happening? I cannot believe it.

Peter steps in between us and puts his hands on our shoulders. The apostles kneel in a circle while Peter prays. "Lord, you know everyone's heart. Show us which one of these two You have chosen to take place in this ministry and apostleship from which Judas turned aside to go to his own place."

Joseph and I step back when it is decided in order to eliminate the influence of man in this decision; lots are cast by the apostles, leaving it wholly in the hands of God. Unable to see the result, Joseph and I cannot stand still while we wait as each lot is cast.

The apostles all stand as Peter moves toward us with a smile. He turns us to where we are facing the crowd. My whole body is trembling as everyone's eyes are watching us. "I wish both of these men could be appointed to the apostleship because both of them are deserving. But Jesus only chose twelve apostles, so we must keep that number the same."

The room is silent as everyone awaits the announcement. "After prayer and casting lots to determine the replacement of Judas Iscariot, the lot falls on...Matthias."

The blood rushes from my head. I feel light-headed and have trouble catching my breath. I lean over with my hands on my knees and almost topple over. Peter's hand catches me by the shoulder, and he pulls me close. "Congratulations, Matthias. You deserve this. Welcome to the Twelve."

When I regain my balance, the other apostles are hugging me and congratulating me as I am jostled from one to the next. Everything is a blur.

I wish my parents could be here to share this experience with me, but maybe I can see them soon and tell them. At least I do have one family member here—Joseph...Joseph is here. He must be disappointed he was not chosen. I am sad for him.

I turn to give him a consoling hug, but he grabs me around the neck. "You have earned this, my friend. You believed and were convicted to the cause long before I was. You have experienced much more than I have. Yes, we walked basically the same path together, but I am not going anywhere. We are a team, and I will be beside you wherever you go. Congratulations!"

He gives me another tight hug before I am turned to be congratulated by the next person. Micah grabs us both around the necks. "Well done, you two. Your family—our family—will be very proud of both of you when they hear this news."

# A MIGHTY WIND

Jewish pilgrims from throughout the Roman region and beyond have gathered in Jerusalem for this festival at the Courtyard of Jewish men in the Temple. Today is the fiftieth day after Passover, thus beginning the two-day celebration of Shavuot or Feast of Weeks—the celebration of God giving the Torah to the Jewish people on Mount Sinai. On Passover, leaven is removed from the bread, but on Shavuot, new leaven is used. I am looking forward to having leavened bread again—it is much tastier. We celebrate the freedom from bondage on Passover, and on Shavuot celebrate the delivery of the commandments by God on Mount Sinai of how to live as people of God. In other words, remove the leaven of old days of slavery of Egyptian suppression and influence and add the leaven of the new commandments of God for His people.

As the scriptures are being read about the thunder and lightning, the thick cloud of smoke on the mount, the fire, the voice of God on Mount Sinai issuing the commandments, a rush of mighty wind fills the room where we are sitting and forms a whirlwind in the middle of the room. That is odd. Where is it coming from?

Unable to move, I stare as a cloven tongue of fire sits upon me. I have a burning sensation in my chest, but it is not painful. Am I dreaming? My chest heaves as I gulp for air as the whirlwind ceases and the fire disappears. What is happening to me?

I turn to the stranger sitting beside me. "Did you see that?"

The thin Egyptian man says he did not see anything, and we start conversing. Joseph has been sitting behind me and taps me on the shoulder. With eyebrows raised, he stutters, struggling to get out the words, "Wh-when did you learn t-to speak Egyptian?"

With palms up and shrugging, I cock my head. "What do you mean?"

"You were just talking to that man in Egyptian. When did you learn to speak it?"

I shake my head and am even more confused when I look around the room. Some of the apostles and believers are talking in the foreign tongues of those beside them. Others are still dazed.

I hear the words of Jesus in my head, "Go into all the world and teach the Gospel."

Then it dawns on me. The believers have received the gift of the Holy Spirit like Jesus promised. What a perfect day for this to happen—on the Day of Mattan or Day of the Gift. The day Israel is celebrating the gift of God's instructions to His people from Mount Sinai in a cloud of smoke and fire is the day we are receiving the gift of the Holy Spirit by cloven tongues of fire to spread His word. And everyone hears it in their own language.

Some in the crowd are amazed at what is happening, while others think we are drunk. They do not realize we can hear and understand every word they say.

Peter stands and motions for all the apostles (it is strange that the elite group includes me now) to join him as he speaks. "Fellow Jews and all who are visiting Jerusalem. Listen carefully while I explain what has just occurred. These people are not drunk, as many of you suspect. It is mid-morning. There has not been time to get drunk." Some in the crowd laugh.

"We are drunk on the Holy Spirit—not wine. This is what was spoken by the prophet Joel. 'I will pour out my Spirit upon all flesh... and they shall prophesy. And whosoever shall call on the name of the Lord shall be saved.'"

"Men of Israel, listen carefully. Jesus of Nazareth, a man thoroughly accredited by God to you by miracles, wonders, and signs which God did through Him, you yourselves know. This innocent and holy man was handed over to you by God's set purpose and foreknowledge, and you, with the help of wicked men, had Him humiliated, tortured, and put to death by nailing Him to a Roman cross. However, God raised Him, our Messiah, from the dead on the third day as was prophesied, freeing Him from the agony of death because it was impossible for death to keep its hold on Him." Many in the crowd squirm, realizing their guilt.

"Our patriarch David died and was buried. But he was a prophet and knew God promised one of his descendants would be placed upon God's throne. David spoke of the resurrection of Christ and said He would not be abandoned to the grave nor His body decay. God has raised this Jesus to life, and we are all witnesses to that fact. Exalted to the right hand of God, He has received from the Father the promised Holy Spirit and has poured out what you now see and hear."

"Hmph," comes sounds from a few in the room who disagree, but that does not even get a reaction from Peter.

"Therefore, let all Israel be assured that God has made Jesus, who you crucified, both Lord and Christ."

Most of the crowd are moved and realize their guilt. A few feel the opposite and leave.

"We killed an innocent man. What shall we do?" comes a question from the crowd.

Peter looks at the man who asked the question. "Repent and be baptized in the name of Jesus Christ for the forgiveness of your sins, and you will receive the gift of the Holy Spirit. For Adonai, God our Father, so loved us that He sent Jesus, the Messiah—His only begotten Son born of the virgin Mary—that whosoever believes He suffered, died on the cross, and was raised from the dead on the third day should not suffer eternal punishment but have everlasting life. Believe this and be baptized, and you will be saved."

"I want to be baptized."

"So do I."

"Baptize me. I want to be forgiven."

The comments echo throughout the room, and a massive group follows us out the southern entrance of the Temple, where there are numerous mikvah, the pools where worshipers ceremonially cleanse themselves before entering the grounds of the Temple. There must be close to three thousand people when I look back over my shoulder. The twelve of us lead the assemblage into the water, and I watch Peter as he baptizes the first person. The other apostles and I copy his example and begin baptizing each person in line.

James, the brother of Jesus, is next in line, and I greet him with a hug. "I should have let my brother baptize me while He was on earth. But I was stubborn and did not want to acknowledge Him as the Messiah. I always knew He was different—in fact, He never did anything wrong as a child or adult and was always wiser than any of us. I guess I was jealous of Him because he never got into trouble. I am sorry it took so long for me to recognize Him. Seeing Him resurrected from the dead, especially after such a horrible death, convinced me He is who He claimed to be—our Messiah."

It takes several hours for us to baptize everyone, and I am exhausted but ecstatic.

As an apostle now filled with the Holy Spirit, I have performed my first official duty—spreading the Gospel to all the world by baptizing new believers in the name of the Father, the Son, and the Holy Ghost.

# THE HOMECOMING

While in Jerusalem, we continue to meet at Solomon's Colonnade in the outer court of the Temple courts daily. Some of the believers share their food and homes with each other since some have sold their property and possessions to help the needy. Day after day, more and more people from Jerusalem and those visiting from surrounding areas are being saved and baptized.

The number of new believers almost double after Peter and John heal a man who has been lame since birth. The people inside the Temple recognize him as the man they had passed moments earlier begging for money as they entered the Beautiful Gate. He is leaping for joy and praising God and making such a commotion that the crowd gathers around him, wanting to know how he is now able to walk. The excited man clings to Peter and John. "These two men healed me."

Peter takes this opportunity to witness and delivers a message much like the one he gave at Shavuot. This time he converts over five thousand people. The Sanhedrin do not like what they see and have Peter and John arrested and kept them overnight. For fear of the crowd of believers, the members of the ruling body order them to stop teaching about Jesus but release the two of them even though they announce they will not quit.

Because of the large numbers of new believers from across the Roman Empire, the apostles are being bombarded with requests to come teach about the Messiah and provide leadership for the new converts—they do not know what to do next. To determine what needs to be done, a meeting is held with "The Twelve" and some of the disciples who followed Jesus when He was present on earth who have remained in Jerusalem.

Peter heads the discussion and identifies the areas where the requests are from so the apostles can choose where they would like to go. After several apostles voice their preferences, Peter asks who volunteers to go to Cappadocia and along the coast of the Caspian Sea. No one volunteers. He looks at me. "Matthias, you speak some Greek, don't you?" I nod yes. "Would you be willing to go there?"

"I would rather stay close to home and my family than to go that far away. But if that is where I am needed, that is where I will go."

Peter smiles. "That is the attitude we should all have. Thank you."

He shifts his attention away from the apostles and to the other disciples in the room. "Although we are going to face opposition and possible arrest or death in some of these places, we have too many requests for the apostles to handle alone. We are going to have to utilize some of you disciples who have been following Jesus throughout most of His ministry and are knowledgeable of the Messiah's teaching, and are willing to witness to the masses. But how do we decide who goes where? We need some of you to volunteer in these areas."

The first place Peter identifies is the Bethsaida area. Joseph stands, and our eyes meet. "I know I told you I would be with you wherever you go." He swallows hard. "But since someone is needed there, I would like to offer to teach in that area."

It will be hard not to have Joseph with me. We have been beside each other ever since we were toddlers. But at least he will be close to the family and be able to help them when needed. I give him a nod of approval. "You have my blessing."

When all the assignments are made, and the meeting is over, I approach Peter. "Before I go to Cappadocia, I would like to visit my parents. I have not seen them since Passover and would like to spend some time with them."

"Of course, that will be fine. Anyway, it is not far off the route you will be taking to Cappadocia. Go and have a nice visit with them."

Since the apostles are going in all directions, it is difficult to say goodbye to them. Especially after traveling alongside them these past several years and living through what we have together. It is possible we may never see each other again. Even saying goodbye to Joab is emotional—he has been a wonderful host throughout this experience.

Joseph and I go visit Micah and Nava before we leave for Bethsaida. Having been in Jerusalem for this extended period of time has given me the opportunity to get to know them better. I will miss them, too. I repeat the warning Jesus gave us about the destruction of Jerusalem and not to tarry there when they see the warning signs. Hopefully, they will not have to worry about it, though. Nava provides us with several loaves of fresh bread, some smoked fish, and fruit...enough to last the entire trip.

We exit the city through the eastern gate and head north alongside the Kidron Valley...just like the night Jesus was betrayed. That seems like ages ago, but it has only been a few months. I look back at the city one last time as we ascend the Mount of Olives. What a beautiful place with so many wonderful people being misled by the pious religious leaders. Hopefully, they will see the Light before it is too late. Will the city really be destroyed and left in ruins, like Jesus said? He has not been wrong about anything else.

Knowing this is probably the last journey Joseph and I will take together for a long time, if not forever, makes me want to make this trip last as long as possible. But I am excited to see my parents—we have not seen each other since they returned home after the Passover and before I was made an apostle. Throughout this trip, Joseph and I talk almost constantly, sharing childhood memories as well as our travels with Jesus and His followers. Heeding Benjamin's warning from our first business excursion to Jericho, we travel in caravans each day and try to find the ones we think will go the fastest and farthest in a day. We make the journey in only six days, which normally takes seven or eight for most people.

When we get to Gergesa, we know we are almost home and quicken our pace as we follow the shoreline of the Sea of Galilee to

Bethsaida. We arrive at the family compound, and Mother is lighting the oil lamp and putting it on the window sill when she sees us. She screams loud enough for Seba, Martha, Benjamin, and Elizabeth to hear. "The boys are here! The boys are here!" They all come running from their houses to greet us.

Mother grabs me around the neck, and I swing her around, lifting her off the ground with her feet flying in the air. Abba must wait for me to put her down before he hugs me. He squeezes me tightly. "I understand it came down to the two of you to replace Judas Iscariot." He reaches over and hugs Joseph. "Congratulations to both of you. That is quite an honor."

"Unfortunately, they could only name one, but I am happy for Matthias. He deserves it. Plus, I get to stay and minister in this area."

Abba tilts his head. "And where will you be, son?"

"I wish I could be closer, but I will be in Cappadocia helping the new believers in that area. They are eager to learn more about Jesus and need guidance on how to worship Him."

"How long will you be there?"

I take a deep breath because I know my parents are not going to like my answer. "There is no set schedule. It could be weeks... months...years. I will be there as long as I am needed."

Mother places her hand on my shoulder. Her chin trembles as she looks through tears into my eyes. "Matthias, we need you, too. What about us?"

I pull her to me and embrace her. "Mother, it will take a while for me to get here from Cappadocia, but I will come as quickly as I can if you need me. People around the world must know they can have everlasting life if they know Jesus as their Savior. Joseph and I are now both messengers of His gospel and must continue the work Jesus began, only Joseph will be here, and I will be farther away. We are both obeying the last words we heard Jesus say as He ascended into the clouds."

Everyone takes a double glance at me as Benjamin responds, "He did what?"

"Jesus took us to the Mount of Olives one last time before He ascended into heaven. He slowly rose from the ground and kept rising until He disappeared into the clouds out of our sight. As He was rising, He commanded us to go into the world and preach the Gospel. So that is what I must do—as an apostle and follower of Christ. The apostles and some of Jesus' disciples are going into different parts of the Roman empire because of the increase in believers since His resurrection and ascension."

Abba raises his eyebrows and purses his lips. "Won't that be dangerous?"

"Maybe, but that is a chance each of us must take. Jesus suffered and died for you and me—so all of us could spend eternity in Heaven. We must not only worship Him with our lives but our lips as well. It is better to die spreading His gospel than to go about our daily lives as if nothing has happened. The world must know, and I, for one, am going to spread the good news and accept whatever my fate may be for doing so."

Mother muffles a sob but says nothing. Abba pulls us both to him in a warm embrace. "I think I speak for your mother when I say this. We are proud of you, son, and your commitment to the cause. Being separated from you over such a distance is difficult enough for us, so please be careful and try to avoid danger. We cannot lose you." Mother sobs.

The next few days with my family pass quickly, and each day is more emotional than the previous one for my parents and me—we all know I must leave for Cappadocia and begin ministering there. I know I will be welcomed by the believers there, but pagan religion has a deep hold upon much of the population, so I do not know how I will be received by them. Am I scared of what might happen? Yes, but I cannot let my fear interfere with the ministry of Christ.

And I cannot let my parents see my apprehension, especially my mother.

My last night at home is filled with laughter and tears as stories from the past are shared by all. The women have made an elaborate feast – roasted lamb, latkes, matzah ball soup, asparagus, and the braided bread challah. Joseph, our fathers, Benjamin, and Daniel climb the ladder to the roof to spend the night. Our conversation lingers well into the night before they drift off to sleep. Between the dread of leaving my family, not knowing when or if I will ever see them again, and the anxiousness of being among new people in a new land, sleep will not come. The sun finally begins to crest above the rooftops.

Joseph and I have been through so much together; it is difficult to say goodbye to him—we have been together since infancy. We cry on each other's shoulders as the rest of the family watches. After hugging everyone else, I am sobbing like a little child by the time I have to bid my parents farewell—and they are, too. I hold onto them as long as I possibly can. I do not know if I can leave them. But I must.

I slowly turn and take a few steps but stop and spin around. Mother runs to me for one last hug and smothers me with kisses. I choke back a strangled sob as Abba envelops us in his arms. I gradually push them away and run as far and as fast as I can down the dirt path without looking back. I must get away—otherwise, I will never leave.

# MY TESTIMONIAL

My instructions are to meet Theophilus at the first house as I enter the village in Cappadocia. By the time I climb the rugged mountain to the volcanic plateau, the sun is just above the horizon. I approach a group of men outside the home, and knowing I am a stranger, they look at me curiously as I draw closer into speaking range.

"Shalom. Peace be with each of you." I look from face to face. "I am Matthias and am here to see Theophilus. He is expecting me."

A smile forms on one man's face. "I am Theophilus, but you may call me Theo. My friends do." He turns to the other men. "This is the man from Jerusalem we have been waiting for. He was a follower of Jesus, the Messiah, and is one of the twelve apostles." He introduces the other men then shifts his gaze to me. "We have been looking forward to your arrival and excited to hear about your experiences as a disciple. But you must be tired and hungry. You will be staying at my home so come with me. My wife, Sofia, will make you something to eat... and you may get some rest."

Theo is a little taller and thinner than I am and takes long strides compared to me—probably from going up and down the mountainside. He has curly dark hair and a close-cut beard. He introduces me to Sofia, who is also tall and thin with long wavy hair that hangs to her waist. Both are probably in their early thirties. There are no children around, so I assume they have none.

Although seasoned differently than I am used to, the food is similar. Sofia has made a pot of chicken stew with homemade bread with some olives and cheese. Pleasantly full, I lay on the mat they provide for me to sleep on and am soon sound asleep.

I am awakened the next morning by a noisy mob outside. Theo tells me I have an anxious audience who began gathering shortly after sunrise waiting to hear me. When the door opens, there must be over a hundred people there. There are cheers as Theo introduces me as an apostle of Jesus, and he tells them all to sit. I stand in the doorway of the house to speak.

"Let me introduce myself. I am Matthias, an apostle of Jesus, and this is my story. Before I saw Him for the first time, my personal life was in shambles. My wife and first-born child, a son, had died during childbirth only a few months earlier, and I was not coping well with their demise. I was having repetitious nightmares of their deaths when I slept and was physically and emotionally exhausted." Several in the crowd sighed sympathetically.

"I was raised in a fishing family and was good at my trade but was unhappy being a fisherman. Especially after the death of a young fisherman close to my age who fell overboard in stormy seas and drowned. His death scraped off the scabs of the old wounds that had not healed, making my life even more miserable. I blamed myself and wondered what I had done to cause all this pain and did not know where to turn. The only way I can describe how I felt is I was lost and alone in a deep and dark emotional pit. That was four years ago, but I am free of the pain now."

"But that is enough about me—let me tell you about meeting and following Jesus. I first saw Him as He was being baptized by John the Baptist in the Jordan River. When I saw Him, I knew He was different...something special. As He was coming up from the river, a dove lit on His shoulder, took a drop of water from His beard, and flew away. Suddenly, a voice echoed from the sky announcing Him as 'My Son, in whom I am well pleased.'"

Several in the crowd speak at once, "Who was speaking?"

"It was the voice of God." There are murmurs from the crowd, but they seem receptive to the explanation.

"Jesus disappeared in the crowd and could not be found. He was not seen by anyone for several weeks, so I did not know what to believe. When He did reappear, rumors began running rampant throughout the area about miracles He was performing. He was healing the sick and had turned six pots of water into wine at a wedding."

This perks everyone's interest, and they stare intently at me, wanting to know the details. I tell them how Benjamin, Joseph, and I went to trade some fish for needed supplies and encountered Andrew, who witnessed the event and confirmed the rumor to be true. I repeat his account of what happened. They are astounded and asking for more. Now I understand what Jesus meant when He said "fishers of men"—they are drawn into the net of believers.

"That night, we went fishing with Andrew and Peter and caught nothing. The next morning as we finished cleaning and storing the nets, Jesus and some of His followers came to us, and Jesus climbed into Peter's boat and ministered to the crowd from the shore. When He finished teaching, He told Peter to launch the boat into the deeper water. None of us wanted to go back out fishing after the disastrous night we had. Plus, we had just finished cleaning and storing the nets and did not want to redo that task so soon. But Peter did as he was told. Jesus said to let down our net, and that is when I witnessed my first miracle by Him. There were so many fish in the net, it began to tear. We called for help from another boat, and the load of fish caused both boats to almost capsize and take on water."

There is more whispering and murmuring among the gathering, but I can see they are still interested. They are leaning in closer with intense gazes to hear the next thing I have to say. Theo hands me a cup of water to wet my throat before I can continue speaking to the enlarging crowd. Several curious people wander up and sit down to hear what I have to say.

"The next time I saw Jesus changed my life forever. Several days later, my uncle Benjamin and I returned to Peter's house. Even though I had been on the boat with Jesus, we were never introduced to each other. This time though, He walked up to me, called me by name, and hugged me. I could not physically move or speak, but the hollowness I had felt since my wife and son's deaths was gone. I felt like a new and different person. That was when I knew for certain He was the Messiah. My uncle, who had suffered a leg injury that continued troubling him after several years, was immediately healed when Jesus hugged him, too. I was healed emotionally, whereas my uncle was healed physically." There is some applause.

I proceed telling them about the many miracles I saw Jesus perform—healing the lame, casting out demons, restoring sight to the blind and hearing to the deaf, and cleansing the lepers. There are oohs and ahs as I describe each miracle. When I tell them about Jesus taking five loaves and two small fish and feeding five thousand people, several begin talking among themselves about how they would like to have been there. Others are shaking their heads in wonder or skepticism—I am not sure which.

Theo stands. "Speaking of food, let's take a break so we can all get something to eat and let Matthias get some rest. He can resume his story in a little while...is about an hour good for you, Matthias?" I nod my head.

I look back as I enter the house and many in the crowd remain seated—they are not going anywhere. Others are rushing toward their homes. Sofia quickly puts two loaves of bread and cheese on the table with some cherries, apricots, and sliced melon. I quickly devour mine and feel energized but stay inside the house until everyone has time to return.

There are even more people gathered outside when we walk out the door. Many of those who stayed have moved closer—we could touch each other if we wanted to. Theo introduces me again for the sake of the newcomers.

"I have told you about many of the miracles Jesus performed, and there are others I will get to at another time. I will tell you about this one, though—I wish I had witnessed this one because it is unbelievable." The assembly remains motionless as I tell them about Jesus walking on the stormy sea. A few of their mouths fall open when I tell them Peter walked on the water, too...at Jesus' command. Most sit silently with hands covering their mouths and looking at one another in disbelief. With confused looks on their faces, others ask how that is even possible.

"The miracles were to glorify God and show His power. If we knew how to do things like that, they would not be miracles, would they? How did Jesus do any of the miracles? It is only for God to know." I pause to let the thought sink in.

"Because of His miracles and the number of followers He had, the Pharisees and Sadducees were losing favor with the Jewish nation because He never fell for any of the traps they tried to set up. They were being humiliated by Him and looked foolish in front of the public." I tell them about several encounters with the Pharisees and Sadducees and their threats against Jesus and His followers. How they even threatened and banished individuals from the synagogues if they proclaimed Jesus to be the Son of God using the once-blind man as an example.

"The religious leaders did what? Why?"

"Their power and influence were publicly challenged by Jesus, and, like I said, they felt they were losing the support of the masses, especially since He had so many followers. Jesus taught peace, humility, and forgiveness—not war, but many thought Jesus would lead a rebellion against the Roman government, and the Jewish ruling body did not want to lose their influence with them. They were the ones who schemed to have Jesus crucified—they felt it was better for one man to die instead of the nation being destroyed." Many shake their heads, not believing the Jewish ruling body could resort to such an act.

Before telling them about the trials and the crucifixion, I list the prophecies Jesus had fulfilled up to that point in His ministry. I then give a detailed description of His prayers at Gethsemane, His betrayal by Judas Iscariot, who I replaced, His Jewish and Roman trials, His torture at the hands of the lictors and Roman guards, and His crucifixion. The eyes of many in the crowd glisten with tears while some bury their faces in their hands at the way He was treated. Some of the men rend their robes as the Jews do in mourning. Some cry out in pain. I did not expect this reaction, so I wait a while before telling them the good news of His resurrection. I want them to think about and appreciate what Jesus endured for the sins of the world.

"There is hope, my friends. Jesus conquered death and physically rose from the dead on the third day and appeared to a group of us in an upper room in Jerusalem. He walked on this earth for forty days afterward. He led us back to the Mount of Olives, and I watched Him ascend into the clouds to sit on the right hand of God our Father in Heaven. I witnessed it all."

I then complete the list of prophecies fulfilled by His crucifixion, resurrection, and ascension. "Believe Jesus is the Messiah—that He suffered and was crucified, conquered sin and death, and is now sitting at the right hand of God the Father so that we may be forgiven of our transgressions and have everlasting life. Be baptized in the name of the Father, the Son, and the Holy Ghost."

"Baptize me!"

"I want to be baptized!"

"Forgive me, Father! I want eternal life!"

Theo has tears running down his cheeks. "I need to be cleansed of my sins, Matthias. Baptize me."

I put my arm around his shoulder. "Lead the way to the river."

Although it is late afternoon, everyone follows Theo and me to the river after I announce I am about to baptize anyone who is interested. Many of them line the shore to watch while Theo and a few others follow me into the calm water. The water is quite a bit cooler here in the mountains than what I am accustomed to in the Sea of Galilee, but I slowly wade into it and become acclimated to the chill. I begin baptizing the new believers...first is Theo, followed by his wife. I continue until the last person is baptized, and not a single individual has left even though the sun is setting behind the trees and the cool dusk wind begins to blow. Everyone is wet and shivering, but they hug their new brother in Christ and greet the last person just the same as they did the first—everyone who followed me here has been baptized.

I shudder as the cool breeze sends shivers up my spine as I exit the water. "Brothers and sisters, welcome to the family of Christ."

The crowd applauds and embraces their neighbors with love and the joy of knowing Christ as their Saviour. "Shalom. Peace be with you all as you go to your homes. Now grow in grace and in the knowledge of our Lord and Saviour. To Him be glory and honor now and forever. Amen."

The crowd disperses, and by the time we get to the home of Theo and Sofia at the edge of the village, a huge orange moon is rising in the eastern sky above the rocky terrain. Theo rests his hand on my shoulder as we stop and stare at its glow before entering the house. Tears fill my eyes while I wonder if my parents are outside seeing this heavenly sight at the same time as I am.

The moon continues to rise, gradually turning into a white glowing ball. A cloud passes in front of it causing the beams of moonlight to separate into thin streams of light to the ground. "Thank you, Father, for Your creation, for the sacrifice of Your Son, and for allowing me to be Your apostle and messenger to introduce new followers into Your family—our family—like the ones who were baptized today. Amen."

We walk inside.

# EPILOGUE

The only time Matthias is mentioned in the Bible is in the book of Acts Chapter 1 when he and Joseph called Barsabbas (also known as Justus) are proposed to fill the position vacated by Judas Iscariot after he hanged himself for betraying Jesus. The apostles cast lots, and the lot falls on Matthias to become one of The Twelve.

Little is known about Matthias, other than that. The tradition of the Greeks says he planted the faith around Cappadocia and along the coasts of the Caspian Sea and lived near the port of Issus. He was beheaded with an ax in Colchis by the pagans there. According to some historians, he first preached the Gospel in Judaea, then in Aethiopia, where he was stoned to death. Others have him preaching to cannibals in the area of Aethiopia, where he died and was buried near the Temple of the Sun. And even some historians have him being stoned in Jerusalem and beheaded while others have him dying of old age there. So, the only real fact we know about Matthias is he was a follower of Christ from baptism to ascension and became the twelfth apostle as "the replacement" to Judas Iscariot.

I do not claim to be a Bible scholar. The chronological order of events of the ministry of Jesus on earth in this book is strictly from my own independent Bible study of the four gospels and the first two chapters of Acts. After establishing what I thought was the sequence of events, I looked at several sources to see how my timeline compared to others and realized that none of the sources agreed one-hundred percent with each other or mine, so if the order of events in this book agrees with any Bible scholar, it is strictly by coincidence.

To enhance my study and make it more meaningful and realistic for me, I created an identity for Matthias and Joseph since nothing is known about either one—except both were disciples of Christ from His baptism to His ascension, and neither was one of the original twelve apostles. I wanted to experience the emotions, beliefs, and/or doubts of what it must have been like to follow Jesus throughout His earthly ministry, so through the eyes of "my" Matthias, this Biblical fiction book is the result of my personal journey as I took on the cloak of Matthias and walked in his sandals with the promised Messiah.

I hope it has been as meaningful and a blessing for you to read as it has been for me to write.

For God so loved the world, that He gave His only begotten Son, that whosoever believeth in Him should not perish, but have everlasting life. For God sent not His Son into the world to condemn the world, but that the world through Him might be saved.

John 3:16–17 (King James Version)